PILLOW TALK WILL GET YOU KILLED 2

BY: CARYN LEE

PILLOW TALK WILL GET YOU KILLED 2

- Written by -

CARYN LEE

Copyright © 2018 by Author Caryn Lee

Published by Author Caryn Lee

Second Edition

Facebook: https://www.facebook.com/caryndeniselee?fref=ts

Cover design/Graphics: Justin Young

Acknowledgments

Writing a book isn't easy, but I never stopped. Here I am ten books later and still writing. Thank you God for giving me the courage to overcame my fear. Thank you to everyone who has encouraged me to achieve my goals. If it wasn't for such a loyal support system I would've never started at book one. To my family, thank you for supporting me. You're the first to hear my ideas, telling everyone that I write books and also purchasing them. To the readers, thank you for supporting me. You one click and shout me out! You post my books on your page! You give me reviews! You show up at the book signings! You purchase my eBooks and paperbacks! You guys are everything! What I want you to know is that you encourage me tremendously. From the bottom of my heart I appreciate you all! Now y'all got me crying (I'm such a crybaby). Please enjoy my characters and my 10th book, "PILLOW TALK WILL GET YOU KILLED 2!"

Chapter 1

Emani

"They have Tyshawn! No! No! No! This is not supposed to be fucking happening!" I paced back and forth in the abandon building.

Ty had a surprised and deranged look upon his face." What the fuck are you saying? I thought you said Tyshawn was at the neighbor's house?" Ty grabbed me forcefully causing my towel to drop to the ground.

I scrambled to pick my towel up, wrapping it back around my body. "Get your fucking hands off me Ty! All of this is your fucking fault, now they have our son!"

"Fuck all that dumb shit that you're talking about. What they fuck did they say on the phone?" Ty asked.

"They want me in exchanged for Tyshawn. They fucking want me instead or else he's dead in twenty-four hours. I can't let them kill my baby." I cried falling to the ground.

Ty took off his shirt putting it on me. "They're not going to kill our son. Chill out, I have a plan." Ty picked me up from the ground.

He carried me to the truck parked in the alley. We couldn't go back to our house. Ty whipped up the alley and hit the corner of our block. It was police and news trucks surrounded around our home. He drove by slowly as we watched the action from afar. I cried in the passenger seat of the car. He rubbed my thigh trying to comfort me. I've been best friends with Tichina for such a long time. I trust that she wouldn't let Tavion harm her God son. Ty received a phone call from someone. I listened to his remarks. What I heard him say next caught me off guard.

"You did what Ty?" I yelled as he was on the phone with the caller.

"Let me hit you right back." Ty told the caller on the phone.

"Please tell me that you didn't kill Tichina! Please tell me that my ears are deceiving me."

"Look I did what the fuck I had to do. What the fuck that you think? That this is a game? Fuck your friend! She wasn't a friend when she sent her nigga and his people to our home. Therefore, the bitch had to get it." Ty replied angrily.

I just remained quietly as I tried to collect all my thoughts. I was seconds away from snapping off and losing it. Ty continued to drive on 290 going west. The only thing that I could think about was Tyshawn. My cellphone rang continually as we drove on the expressway. I know that everyone was calling me regarding the incident at my home. I received a call from Big Momma. I answered whimpering on the phone.

"Emani child what the hell is going on? The police are outside my house. Please tell me that you're okay. Emani please say something." Big Momma said.

"Please don't let them take my children away. The less you know, the better. I love you Big Momma." **Click**. I put my phone on vibrate.

Grabbing the neck of the shirt, I wiped away the tears and snot from my face. Ty looked at me with a mean expression on his face. I turned my head away looking out the window remaining quiet the reminder of the ride. Two hours later we pulled up to a gated complex of homes. Ty pulled in a code and the gate opened. He pulled in driving pass the beautiful homes until we reached the cul-de-sac. Ty opened the garage that was connected to the home entering it. He parked inside, hopped out grabbing a black duffle bag out the trunk. He walked over to my side opening the door for me.

"Welcome home." He helped me out of the truck.

I followed behind him inside, everything was beautiful. I looked around the partially furnished home. "Where are we?" I asked Ty.

"Sugar Grove, go upstairs and look around your new home." Ty instructed.

Slowly I walked toward the spiral staircase. I knew that Ty promised me a new beginning, but I wasn't expecting anything like this. When I made it up the stairs there were four huge bedrooms. The master bedroom was the only one that I was interested in now. It already had a bedroom set inside. The bed was made. I looked around at the other three bedrooms. They were the same, furniture included. Ty was sitting in our bedroom on the plush beige carpet counting the money from the duffle bag. I took of the dirty shirt preparing to take a shower.

"Ty the house is beautiful, but we need to get Tyshawn back before they kill him." I said.

"Emani chill I already got someone working on that. Do you think that I would actually allow them pussy ass niggas to kill our son?" Ty wackily smiled. He laughed as he continued to count the money. "Go ahead and take a shower and slip into something nice. Relax, your man got this."

Following his commands, I did what I was instructed to do. As I took my shower I thought about Tyshawn and begun to cry. I was concerned about Tichina parents How could Ty kill Tichina without first discussing anything with me. I stepped out the shower to my buzzing. Ty left the room, maybe he was downstairs. I picked up my phone, it was Big Momma calling again. This time I could speak to her.

"Hello Big Momma." I said.

"Child, are you safe? The police questioned me for an hour. They said that your house was involved in a shooting and that they're looking for you and Ty. I also heard that Tichina has been shot multiple times and fighting for her dear life. What's going on Emani?"

"Big Momma I can't really say too much over the phone. How are my children, are they fine?" I asked.

"Yes, they're safe with me. Has Ty threaten you Emani, making you do anything against your own will?" Big Momma asked me sounding concerned.

"Big Momma I'm fine can you please put Lil Ty and Tyeisha on the phone for a second?"

Big Momma put my children on the phone. They were concerned about what was going on too. "Listen I'm going to send an Uber for you and sister and have them bring you to me and your father. Put Big Momma back on the phone." I told them.

"Big Momma praying mama. You know that we can't disturbed Big Momma while she's praying." Lil Ty said.

"Okay that's fine. I'm about to send an Uber now, get ready." I quickly ended the call and ordered my children an Uber.

Ty walked into the room still counting money. "Who was that on the phone?"

"Big Momma telling me what's going on, I'm sending for Lil Ty and Tyeisha to come home. I don't feel comfortable with them being in the city. Bad enough they already have Tyshawn."

Ty phone started to ring, he ignored everything that I just said. Honestly, I don't think that he heard me. He walked off with the money in his hands into the other room. Seconds later he walked back inside the room. I was sitting on the bed in a daze.

"I'm going to handle some business. You have food downstairs, we don't have cable yet but we do have Wi-Fi so you can watch Netflix." Ty walked into the closet to grab some all black to put on. He changed into his all black clothing and grabbed a black ski mask. I asked him several questions but he didn't bother to answer me. He walked out of the room, down the stairs, proceeding to leave out of the house.

"Ty what's going on? So you're just going to leave me hanging and not tell me shit! What are you going to do about Tyshawn?!" I ran down the stairs behind him.

5

Ty grabbed me by the waist. "Emani you're safe here, far out and no one knows where we are. I hope that you didn't tell Big Momma. I got to get out of here. I promise that I'll get our son back." Ty kissed me on the forehead before leaving out of the door.

He was amped up off something, what it was I didn't know. I checked the navigation on the Uber app to see where my children were at. They were on the way to me. I called Lil Ty's phone to make sure that they were fine. Lil Ty answered saying that they were cool and couldn't wait to see me. My phone continued to ring nonstop as I watched the news. My home shooting was the top story in Chicago. My landlord was being interviewed by the reporters. He didn't have much to say because he didn't know anything. He was angry because of the damage that was done on his property. I cried as I watched the police officers go back and forth into my old home. There was no way that I could go back there ever again. The good news was that Tichina wasn't dead. I decided to make a phone call to Kamara.

I dialed her number, to my surprised she answered. "Please don't hang up Kamara." I wept on the other line.

"What the fuck do you want Emani? You got a lot of mother fucking heart to be calling my phone right now!" Kamara was angry.

"Look I got a phone call saying that they have Tyshawn. Sis can you please make sure that they don't harm my son. I had nothing to do with any of this." I lied threw my teeth and cried harder but Kamara wasn't falling for it.

"Sis, I'm not your damn sister or best friend. Emani you allowed Ty to manipulate you into crossing your own friend. How could you? After all that we've been through.

Now Tichina is in the hospital fighting for her life and you're worried about your fucking son. Bitch fuck you and your son! What goes around comes the fuck around. You're a dirty bitch!"

"Kamara I promise I had nothing to do with Tichina getting shot. Please you must believe me, you know me better than that." I cried.

"Yeah I know you alright. I know that you've been plotting ever since the beginning against Tavion and his crew. I always knew that Ty was going to be the death of you. All that cut throat and conniving shit that you two been doing all these years is finally catching up with you. Good bye Emani, I hope that you rot in hell right with my baby father!" **Click**.

"Kamara! Kamara! Noooo, please don't hang up!" I yelled into the phone. I called her phone back several times but was sent to the voicemail.

Shit! Why did Ty have to shoot Tichina? I knew for sure that Tavion was ready to kill me, my son and Ty. I cried in a fatal position rocking back and forth. Everything was getting out of control. I had people texting me death threats from numbers that I didn't recognize. People calling me from unknown numbers that I didn't know. Looking at the location of the Uber driver, I saw that he was twenty minutes away. I jumped out of the bed and started rumbling through the dresser drawers. Ty had a few belongings in them, a bunch of bullshit. I scrambled everything around until I found what I was looking for. The small bag of cocaine was underneath his boxers. Greedily I emptied the coke on the dressers to sniff. I needed something to calm my nerves right now. I sniffed two lines allowing that shit to hit me.

"Yes." I said to myself as I took a seat on the floor. The coke worked immediately taking my pain away. I went from crying to smiling in several seconds. High off the dope I started seeing unicorns, clowns, and balloons. I was floating in the sky with the clouds. Picking my cell phone up, I called Big Momma to talk. She answered the phone on the first ring, sounding worried.

"Big Momma they got Tyshawn. The killers, that shot up my house looking for Ty. It was all Ty idea, everything. From the murders to Tichina getting shot." I continued to talk fast, jabbering off at the mouth.

"Emani slow down baby, I don't understand what you're saying." Big Momma replied.

"Big Momma when did you get on the phone." Feeling good and high I started floating again.

The drugs had me high as a kite. I heard the voice of Lil Ty and Tyeisha on the phone next telling me that they were outside the locked gate. Big Momma called my phone back several times, but I didn't answer. Struggling to get up I managed to splash cold water on my face. Before leaving the bathroom, I wanted to make sure that I was appropriate. Those two lines had my mind racing and had me thinking of unbelievable things. As I walked out of the bedroom I grabbed the nine millimeters that was sitting on the dresser. Although I did feel safe out here, but I'd much rather be better safe than sorry.

Chapter 2

Tavion

I stood by Tichina's as she rested. The doctors managed to remove the bullet that was lodged in her chest. The bullet was inches away from her heart. Whoever did this to my baby was going to die. I made sure that Tichina had security surrounded by her room. She was in Mount Sinai trauma unit. Not knocking the great care that they have, but they also employ a lot of shady people from the neighborhood. I received an anonymous phone call as I sat by her bedside.

"Yo." I replied.

"Hello Tavion, you're the man that I'm looking for." The caller said.

I didn't recognize the voice. "Who the fuck is this?!"

"You have someone very special and that's my son. Since you want to grab family members I decided to kidnap someone very dear to your heart."

That's when I realized that the caller was Ty. Seconds later my grandma Pearl voice could be heard on the other line. "Tavion please save me." Grandma Pearl sounded afraid. Ty got back on the phone.

I was furious, ready to kill his ass. "You harm her and will bury your ass!" I threaten Ty.

"No nigga what you will do is drop my son off to me alive along with one hundred thousand dollars. After that you can have your sweet granny back. Meet me by the garbage disposal by the train tracks on Kostner or your granny is dead." **Click.**

Fuck these niggas didn't know have an idea who they were fucking with. I pulled over one of my partners over to the side telling them what just went down. Just then Tichina's parents walked inside the hospital room. They both looked upset with me.

"Hello Mrs. Jefferson." I spoke. Mrs. Jefferson walked passed me silently.

"Hello Tavion." Mr. Jefferson spoke up instead.

Mrs. Jefferson held her daughters hand, bowed her head and begin to pray in silence. Tears rolled down her face as she prayed. I stood off to the side and watched Tichina as she laid in the hospital bed. In a matter of seconds the room went from quiet to loud. Sweet church lady, Mrs. Jefferson turned around to attack me. She tried to wrap her small hands around my neck.

She screamed, "You did this to my daughter! All your drug dealing and drug lifestyle!"

Mr. Jefferson grabbed his wife pulling her off me. "What is your problem? Our daughter is lying here fighting for her life and you want to act a fool." He sat his wife down in the chair on the other side of the room.

I brushed it off, understanding that Tichina's mother was hurt and only taking her pain out on me. Blaming me was easier for her to do. Right now, I didn't really have time to explain the situation to her parents because I had to rescue grandma Pearl. As I prepared to leave, Tichina eyes flinched a few times. We rushed over to her bedside quickly.

"Tichina can you hear me? Her father asked her. Her mother held her hands praying and shouting.

Tichina opened her eyes slowly. She parted her dry lips and mumbled something. I couldn't her or understand what she said.

I turned to her mother shaking her, "Please be quiet." I demanded.

"Sweetheart what did you say?" I asked her.

Tichina mumbled again, "Ty did this."

"Ty, your best friend Emani guy?' I wanted to make sure that's what I heard.

"Yes." Tichina mumbled.

I pulled my phone out making a call. After that I gave instructions to my men. "No one is to leave her alone ever. Do you understand me?!" I told them.

Her parents had a confused look upon their faces. They were trying to figure out what was going on. Preparing to leave, Mr. Jefferson grabbed my arm.

"Wait, what exactly is going on?' He asked me.

"Your daughter just revealed who did this to her." I explained to him.

"Wait are you saying that Emani has something to do with this?" Mrs. Jefferson asked.

"Emani has a lot to do with this. More than you would ever know." I replied and left the room.

***

We all met up at the slot before we made our next move. We didn't have much time and was moving fast. Them broke ass niggas had my grandmother. Getting the one hundred thousand wasn't a problem. My grandmother was worth more than that. Today someone was going to die and it wasn't going to be anyone of us. Emani and Ty's nappy headed son was in the back crying complaining that he was hungry. Their son could starve to death, I don't give a fuck. Dee walked inside and joined us. I filled him in on what was going on.

"That nigga isn't getting no money. I mean you can bag it up, but no one is coming out alive." Dee angrily replied.

My solider brought me the cash and the little boy. We all left out, I already had two shooters there checking out the scenery. Keith, Dee and I rode in the truck together. On the ride, there I received a phone call from one of my solders.

"Boss man those pussy niggas just pulled up in two white vans. They're getting out right now and it looks like your grandmother is inside one of the vans. I have a clear shot on all of them. You just give us permission we can drop all of them." My solider informed me.

"Not yet it's too risky. I know that you see us pulling in now. I'll tell you to make the move after I received my grandmother safely." I replied.

"10, 4. Boss man." **Click**.

We pulled up as Ty and two other niggas stood outside.
The two other men were wearing black ski masks and
dressed in all black. His son reached out crying for his
father when he seen him. As I stepped out of the truck my
hand was planted on my desert eagle. I grabbed the bag of
money and started to walk toward Ty.

"Where is my grandmother? I asked Ty through clenched
teeth.

Ty looked at the masked men that were with him nodding
his head. One of the masked men walked over to the van
pulling my grandmother out roughly. She was blindfolded,
her mouth was covered with duct tape and her hands were
tied together with a rope. Filled with rage I aimed my gun
at Ty.

"Yo don't want to do that playboy. Just hand over my son
and the cash and nobody will get hurt." Ty smirked and
said.

I wanted to blow this nigga head off but the masked men
had the gun pointed at my grandmother head. It was too
risky to take a shot. His bratty son continued to cry.

"My grandmother first then the cash." I requested.

He pushed my grandmother toward me causing her to fall
to the ground. With one hand on the bag of money, Ty
snatched it out of my hands. Dee fired the first round of
shots hitting Ty. We all started shooting, including my
people firing from their area. I shielded my grandmother as
she ran back to get inside the truck. Ty and his people ran
off toward their vans. A freight train was headed in our
direction. You can hear the alarms and see the lights

flashing as the gates were lowered. We fired several rounds at the vans as they pulled off driving toward the train tracks. They managed to make it in the other side of the tracks before the train hit them.

"Choo! Choo! Choo!" The train horn blew loudly.

My shooters continued to shoot, but didn't have a clear view hitting the train. We all ran getting back into the truck. Grandma Pearl was shaken up a bit, but fine. Keith drove taking over the wheel as sat with my grandmother in the back.

"Fuck! I tried to kill that nigga!" Dee angrily said.

"Don't worry all of them are going to die. Grandma Pearl did you find out anything while they had you?" I asked her.

"No I couldn't hear anything because they stuffed earplugs in my ear. Tavion I can't go back to my home. They barged threw the back door when they snatched me." Grandma Pearl replied.

"Don't worry you can live at my place out of town. I already have someone back at your home taking care of that. You're safe now and will stay at my house out of town." I assured my grandmother.

Keith busted a U-turn because of the train. My solider gave me a phone call before leaving his location. I gave him the green light to go and I will give him a call later. My main priority right now was to get Grand Pearl out of town so that she wouldn't end up dead.

Chapter 3

Tyrese

The train missed my van by an inch. The horn blew loudly, **"Choo! Choo! Choo!"** Maine and Tone were waiting for me parked on the other side of the track. Looking down to see how Tyshawn was doing. I noticed that he was lying flat on the floor and unresponsive.

"Tyshawn! Tyshawn!" I yelled as I shook him several times.

Tyshawn didn't respond, he was bleeding profusely. I panicked as the blood over flowed out of his stomach.

"Damn! Come on son you can't die on me!" I grabbed the nearest thing to wrap up his wound.

Maine rushed over to check out what was going on. "What's up?" Maine asked me. He looked inside the van and saw Tyshawn covered in blood. "Awe shit man, we have to get him to the hospital now!"

"How do I take him to the hospital? What do I tell the police when they start to question me?" I angrily asked Maine.

Tyshawn started to cough up blood and utter sounds. Seconds later my son died before my eyes taking his last breath. His head fell to the side and body went limp.

"Tyshawn No!" I cried.

"Look man we have to go now! The train is about to end." Maine yelled

Tone blew the horn signaling for Maine to hurry up. Maine left me, running back to the van and jumped inside. Tone pulled off leaving me alone to deal with my dilemma. I cried as I held my dead son. What was I supposed to do with his body? I certainly couldn't ride around with his dead body in my van. Only thing that I could think of doing was morally wrong. I picked him up, carrying his dead body to a pile of trash.

"I'm so sorry son. I love you so much." I cried as I hid and covered his dead body in the trash.

The freight train had six cars left. I had to get out of sight fast before someone seen me. It was hard for me to leave my son like that, but I couldn't go to jail for his murder. I took flight whipping my van down Lake Street. Time wasn't on my side so I blew past a couple of red lights. Thinking quickly, I dumped the bullet riddled van in K Town and set it on fire. I footed it back to the trap house carrying the bag of money.

**

When I made it back to the trap house, music was blasting from the speakers of the home theater. Chicago artist Dreezy song, Close To You was playing. Tweety was eating Sweetie's pussy on the couch. They were both enjoying one another that they didn't hear me come in. Sweetie jumped up when she saw me.

"What the fuck happened Ty, you're covered in blood." Sweetie asked.

Tweety jumped from between her legs and stared at me crazy. "Damn I hope that whatever you did they don't come here." She replied.

"Did Maine and Tone stop by here?" I rushed to the bathroom to clean myself off. Sweetie and Tweety followed their naked asses behind me.

"No, they haven't been by here. What's up should we be alarmed about anything?" Sweetie continued to ask.

"Nah everything is cool, just got into a jam that's all. Look I'm going to be out of sight for a while. Hold the place down and continue to do your thing." I changed into so more clothes.

Sweetie and Tweety both eyed the bag at the same time and looked at one another. "What's in the bag Ty?" Tweety asked.

"None of your mother fucking business." I grabbed the bag of money and bloody clothing leaving out the bathroom. I was in rush and had to get the fuck out of the city. Tweety and Sweetie continued to follow me. The whispered something quickly under their breath.

"Ty what are we supposed to do until you get back?' Tweety asked with an attitude.

"Still working on them two niggas that I put you two on. If you're doing your job right, money shouldn't be a problem." I told her ass.

Tweety was the smart one, I had to watch out for her ass. Sweetie simple ass stood next to her quietly waiting for

Tweety to reply. Today I wasn't going back and forth with Tweety thin ass. I left the both standing there as I left out the back door. My white Chevy Impala was parked in the back. They both watched me as I jumped in my whip and sped down the alley. Where the fuck was Maine and Tone? As I rode up Independence, Maine flew past me in his car. He was by himself we made eye contact. When I reached Jackson, I made a right to meet him back at the house. My cell started ringing, it was Maine calling me. I answered quickly and kept it short telling him to meet me at the spot. When I pulled back into the back Maine was already standing outside. Reaching into the duffle bag, I gave him his cut. He looked inside the car before he got inside.

"Here you go, where the fuck is Tone? Where did you dump the van?" I asked.

"Tone got up with his bitch, he'll hit you up for his cut in a minute. I dumped the van on the street. You need to get out of here, you look like shit." Maine replied.

"I'm gone right now. Keep an eye on Tweety and Sweetie and don't tell them shit. I'll be out of sight for a few days. Make sure that everything is straight. Maine what happened back there with my son is between you and me."

"Cool, you can trust me. I got you, hit me up when you ready to make the next move." Maine bailed out of the car.

Resuming back in route to home, I watched out for any suspicious activity. This long fucking ride had me exhausted. The death of Tyshawn was heavy on my mind. I was running out of options and had to come up with a bigger plan. At the rate that everything was going I was going to end up dead. Death wasn't going to happen to me period. With forty minutes left on the road. I received a phone call from someone that I haven't heard from in a long time.

"Yo where the fuck you been?" I barked threw the phone.

"Ty, I've been in hiding. Dee shot me in my arm at Jay's. I checked into the hospital, after they put on my cast I got the fuck out of there. I heard about what happened to your home on the news." Tootie replied.

"Yeah those niggas came for me. I'm cuffed away safely out of the way." I told her as I drove down the highway checking my mirrors.

"Ty my money running low and I have to be out of the hotel by tomorrow." Tootie cried into the phone.

I paused for a second, Tootie cried harder into the phone. Having her close could be a good asset. She knew Tavion more than anyone. With her by my side I could use her and also keep an eye on her.

"Where are you right now?"

"I'm at Red Roof Inn in Arlington Heights." She sniffled.

I told her to meet me at a hotel close by my house. Shit I wasn't going to give her my address. Not wanting to be on the phone for a long time I ended the call.

***

Before going inside the house, I hid the bag of money in the garage behind some boxes. I stepped inside, Tyeisha and Lil Ty were in the kitchen.

"Hey daddy." They gave me a hug. Grabbing their noses the stepped away from me "You smell like gasoline daddy. Where is Tyshawn?" Lil Ty asked me.

I ignored his question. "Where is your mom?"

"She's upstairs in the room." He replied.

I left them cooking in the kitchen to go upstairs. Emani was lying in bed chilling. On the side of her was a bottle of Remy. I took a seat on the edge of the bed, Emani jumped up immediately.

"Ty, you look fucked up. Is that blood behind your ears?" Emani grabbed a napkin off the dresser and wiped the blood off me "Where is my baby, Tyshawn?" she asked me with worried eyes.

"They still have him." I lied to her.

"Ty, you promised that you would handle everything!" Emani punched me in the chest.

I jumped up from the bed, it was the only thing that could keep me from putting my hands on her. "We had a shootout, my men against his men. I was outnumbered by Tavion's men. I was lucky that I made it out alive."

"What the fuck do you mean, you were lucky that you made it out alive? Those niggas have our damn son!" Emani shouted in my face. "Ty, you know that they are savages. Look at what they did to our home just to get to me. They're going to kill my baby boy!" Emani repeated as she paced back and forth.

I grabbed Emani forcefully. Staring at her, traces of white powder covered the tip of her nose. The bitch was high, that explains her actions. Looking at the dresser I seen the two lines of powder that were lined up. Emani read my mind snatching her boy away from me.

"Yes, I'm fucking high! What else am I supposed to do at a time like this? She picked up the glass of Remy and sipped on it.

I was too fucking tired and didn't have time to deal with High Emani. Instead of dealing with her I went into the other bedroom. Right now, I needed to focus on what my next move is going to be. Emani was ranting and raving in the other. She was so loud that I could hear her. My children knocked on the door to tell me that they mother was tripping out. At that moment Tootie called me telling me that she was at the hotel. I told them to go and keep their mother company while I went to make a run. They went in the room distracting their mother as I went to meet up with Tootie. She followed me back to my place and parked her vehicle next to mine in the garage.

"This is such a lovely home Ty. Are you sure that I can stay here with you?" Tootie looked around my home as she stood in the middle of the living room.

I was carrying her bags for her. "It's no problem, follow me I'll show you where you would be sleeping. Tootie followed me upstairs to the spare bedroom. We walked passed my bedroom door where Emani and my children were.

"Wow this is so nice of you, very nice." Tootie plopped down on the queen size bed.

"The bathroom is down the hall and the kitchen is downstairs. I trust that you won't tell anyone where you are. I know all of this is nice, but if I feel any kind of dishonesty I won't hesitate to kill you." I kissed her on the forehead and prepared to walk out the bedroom.

Tootie ran after me, "Wait are you coming back to hang out with me tonight?" her eyes told me that she wanted to fuck.

At that moment, I could hear my children voices. "I'll be back to check on you later." When I opened the door Tyeisha and Lil Ty caught a glimpse of Tootie. I closed the door behind myself quickly.

"Who is that lady in the room daddy?" Tyeisha asked, she was nosy just like her damn mother.

"None of your business nosy rosy. Now you two go on to your rooms. I would've expected that you two would be camped out in your rooms equipped with all your latest gadgets." I walked down the hall to their rooms with them.

"The new house is cool and everything, but we're concerned about mom." Lil Ty replied.

I sat down and had a serious talk with Lil Ty and Tyeisha. As we were talking Emani voice roared through the bedroom walls.

"What the fuck are you doing in my house bitch?" Emani yelled.

Quickly I ran out of the room, by that time Emani was already rushing down the hallway after Tootie. **Boom! Boom! Boom!** Emani banged on the bathroom door. "Hoe if you don't get your hoe ass out of my bathroom now I will kill you!"

"Yo Emani chill baby. Chill I allowed her to stay here until all this shit boils over with." I held Emani back from the door.

"Allowed her to stay here with us? Ty what the fuck is wrong with you? What the fuck are you doing? This is our home, where we lay our heads and you bring the devil who started it all in this bitch!" Emani cried.

"Let me holler at you for a second in the room." I pulled Emani by the arm she tried to resist and get away. That wasn't happening because I was stronger than she was.

"You're out of control Ty for pulling this stunt. You know that I don't rock with her like that. What we did was a onetime thing that I wish that I never did." Emani was livid.

"It's only temporary, besides she can lead us to Tavion." I whispered to her, not wanting our children to hear.

"The only place that she's going to lead us is to death. Ty I'm not feeling any of this bullshit! This all straight bullshit! I don't give a fuck what you do, if you get my baby boy back alive! That bitch better keep her distance away from me!" Emani went to lie down in bed. I proceeded to leave out of the room to see if Tootie was cool. "Aye where do you think you're going?" Emani yelled.

"Chill out, now you're being to extra Emani." I replied before walking down the hall.

Tootie was still in the bathroom taking a shower. I tapped on the door, "It's me, unlock the door." I told her. Tootie unlocked the door, I turned the knob and entered. Her thick chocolate ass was standing there naked. Water was dripping from her body, she was tempting me right now. "You good?" I asked her.

"Yes, I didn't mean to start anything." Tootie licked her lips and grabbed my dick. "So, are you going to sleep with me tonight or her?"

Damn, how could I resist all this chocolate! I thought to myself.

Chapter 4

Kamara

"Karli, are you ready to go baby girl?" I was in my bedroom playing with my hair.

Frustrated, I just put it in a ponytail. Besides right now I was trying to be all cute and shit. Karli and I were on our way to see about Tichina. Her mother called and told me that she was responsive. God knows, I prayed so hard for my best friend ever since I found out. Keith hasn't really been by my house because he was out taking care of business. After throwing my hair in the ponytail I went to go see what was taking my daughter too long to get ready.

"Baby girl, are you ready?" I walked into her bedroom.

Karli was ready and holding a drawing that she made. "I'm ready now momma, this is a drawing that I made for TeTe Tichina."

"This is beautiful Karli." I looked of the drawing. It was purple and pink hearts drawn around 'I Love You'.

We left out of the house and I made sure that I hit the alarm. On the ride to the hospital Keith gave me a call. I had on my Bluetooth earpiece and answered his call.

"Hey bae." I said.

"What's up baby? What are you and Karli doing?" He asked me.

"We are on our way to the hospital to see Tichina right now. What's going on with you? I miss you so much."

"Cool, I heard that she's doing much better. Right now, I'm still taking care of business. I was just calling to check on my two favorite girls. You know making sure that you were okay. I miss you as well. I promise after all of this bullshit is over we're going on a vacation." Keith said.

"You know that I'm worried about you Keith. I can't lose you, you're the best person that has come into my life. I'm praying that God covers you and your friends. I love you." My eyes began to water up. I held the tears back because I didn't want to cry in front of Karli.

"Continue to pray for us beautiful, these streets aren't playing fair. Don't you dare cry on me? Call me when you make it up to the hospital. Tell Karli that I said hello. I love you beautiful."

I blew Keith several kisses before ending the call. Karli was in the car seat playing with her tablet. I told her that Keith said hello and she smiled.

We pulled up to Mount Sinai hospital, it was busy outside. Police cars were parked out front, you would think that you were at a police station. Karli gripped my hand tightly as we walked inside. The security officer at the front door stopped us.

"Excuse me Miss, I have to check you and your bag before you enter." He said.

"Are you serious? Since when do you have to get searched when you visit someone in the hospital?" I rolled my eyes.

Fuck! I had my Beretta on me just in case I had to use it. Now I had to go back to my car to put it up. The female security officer looked at me, "Miss you can step over here, I'll take care of you."

I walked over to her, she seemed cool. She looked inside my Louie bag quickly touching the gun. "You're good, and your daughter is so pretty." She smiled, waving at Karli.

"Thank you so much." I said.

She nodded her head, "No problem, just looking out for a sister."

We walked off and I stopped in the gift shop to buy Tichina some things. I grabbed some flowers and two Get Well balloons. Karli was being my little helper today, she held the balloons in her right hand and the flowers in her left hand. We took the elevator to the Intensive Care Unit. Right now I didn't feel comfortable being here. The smell brought back the moment when I was hospitalized. Upon stepping off the elevators, the ICU was very busy. Already knowing where Tichina room was, I went straight to it. Two big muscled men were standing in front of her door. I already knew that Tavion had provided her with security. They moved out of the way, allowing me and Karli to enter. Tichina was bandage and hooked up to machines. Looking at my best friend in this condition brought me to tears. Karli gave me a hug, wrapping her tiny arms around my waist.

"Don't cry mommy. Auntie Tichina will be okay." Karli softly spoke.

I gathered my feelings together for my daughter sake. Karli released the balloons and gave me the flowers before taking a seat in the empty chair. Tichina didn't deserve this at all. That bitch ass nigga Tyrese and that foul ass bitch Emani was going to pay! As I sat on the side of the bed holding Tichina hand, the tears started up again.

"Don't cry Sis." Tichina slowly said.

I looked up quickly. "Tichina I'm sorry that you're like this." I kissed her on the cheek.

"I'm a fighter you know that I'll get through this." Tichina said.

"Yes you will, shhhh don't talk. You're too weak. I'm here to be by your side. You know that I'll sit here every day by your side Sis." I replied.

The nurse walked into the room to do her job. She took Tichina vitals and gave her medicine. I asked if it was okay to elevate her head slightly. It wasn't a problem, after she was repositioned Tichina looked more comfortable. Now she was able to see Karli. The nurse left us alone and we continued our visit.

"Karli come over and give Auntie a kiss." Tichina said.

Karli hesitated for a minute taking a look at me.

"It is fine Karli, she's not in any pain." I assured her.

Karli scooted the chair closer to the bed, not being afraid. The moment she began to talk she didn't stop. Tichina listened to every summer camp story that Karli told her. We stayed by Tichina's bedside for hours, just kicking it, laughing and talking. It was getting late, I had to feed Karli and get home.

"Tichina I'm leaving now, I'll be back tomorrow afternoon. I love you best friend." I kissed her on the forehead.

Karli gave her God mother a kiss as well. We said good bye to Tavion's men, that we're guarding her door and bounced out of there. It was after seven pm, past Karli bedtime. On the ride home I stopped off to buy Karli and me some tacos. The ride home didn't take long because it wasn't that much traffic on the expressway. I pulled into my garage before nine pm. Before I stepped into my home, I pulled out my Beretta. Karli knew the routine, following behind me. The coast was clear, all of this bullshit going on had me paranoid. I put the code to my alarm in. You never know what Emani next move could be. Whatever that bitch was pulling next I was prepared for that ass. That dirty bitch knew where I lived so had to be ready.

As we sat at the table eating our tacos the nine o clock news came on. Karli was singing a song to her baby doll being a child. The top was a young boy body found on the west side of Chicago. It caught my attention, but I could barely hear the story.

"Karli baby take you and your doll in your bedroom to go play. I'll be in there in a minute to put you to bed." I kissed her on the cheek.

Karli continued to sing walking to her bedroom. I turned the revision up louder so that I can hear.

The news reporter told the story. "Several hours ago a young boy body was discovered in a pile of garbage. Garbage workers were doing their job when they stumbled upon a lifeless body. It appears that the boy was African American, about the age two years old and had a shot wound to the chest. His body has yet to be identified and

Chicago police are now on the case. This is Damara White reporting live from Eyewitness News."

Seconds later I heard keys jingle in my door. I grabbed my Beretta while taking a look my security camera. Keith was entering through the door. I lowered my gun and fingered my hair making sure that it was decent.

"Front door open." The alarm sounded off.

Keith walked inside, put in the code and smiled at me. He looked exhausted and rough.

"Hey baby!" I ran into his arms like a young school girl. "How are you? You look tired. Keith stomach let out a big growl. "Do you want me to cook you something to eat?" I asked him.

Keith squeezed me tightly, giving me a big bear hug. "Baby I'm hungry, tired and horny." He replied.

I giggled. "Those aren't problems at all for me." I looked him in his eyes, kissing him passionately. "Let me put Karli to bed first. I'll take care of you when I'm done."

I went in the room to put Karli to bed. My precious baby girl was asleep in her baby with her baby doll. Karli was knocked out from the long day that we had. I undressed her into her pajamas, tucked her in bed and kissed her on the forehead. Upon stepping back into the hallway, I could hear my shower running. Keith was taking a shower so I busied myself with dinner. Searching in my deep freezer for something to cook. I decided to make him a cheeseburger and fries. I know that it wasn't a Sunday dinner, but it would do. I pulled out my good cast ironed skillets and prepared to cook. While the patties and fries were cooking. I chopped up the lettuce, tomatoes and onions. The television was still telling the death story of the young man. I was distracted by the news that I didn't even hear Keith walk in the kitchen.

"You got it smelling good in hear baby." Keith wrapped his arms around me. He was wearing a white wife beater, some Polo pajama pants and slippers.

I turned to face him. "It's not a Sunday dinner, but I'll hook you up a good ass cheeseburger."

He took a seat at the table. Keith glanced at the television rubbing his goatee. The look on his face triggered off that something wasn't right.

"What is it? Why are you looking at the television like that? I asked him as I looked into his eyes. He remained silent, then it hit me. I started thinking putting two and two together. African American boy about the age of four. "Keith please tell me that it's not." I didn't want to say Tyshawn's name.

Keith gave me a nonchalant look. I slammed the knife down on the kitchen table storming out of the kitchen.

"Baby!" Keith yelled chasing after me.

Quickly I ran into my bedroom crying and pacing the floor back and forth. Everything was fucking crazy right now.

Keith walked into the room. "Look you know that I can't say nothing about what's going on. The less that you know, the better. Besides if you're upset about the death of the little boy, blame his parents."

"Keith he was child that didn't deserve any of this!" I yelled.

"Kamara do you want to wake up Karli?" Keith closed my bedroom door. He lifted my chin up and looked into my eyes. "It's nothing that you can do so don't allow this to upset you." He kissed me on the lips.

"This has been the worst year ever. Why is all this bullshit happening? First my baby father tries to kill me by setting me on fire. Tichina gets shot and now Tyshawn may be dead behind all of this bullshit. I pray that I don't lose you. I can't take any more bad news." I cried

The smoke alarm went off. **Beep! Beep! Beep! Beep! Beep!** "Oh shit the food!" I said.

Keith and I jetted out of the room into the smoked filled kitchen. The food was burnt crisped. I turned off the aye, threw on my pot holders and tossed the burnt skillet in the sink. As I poured water on the skillet, Keith opened up the windows for fresh air. When the fresh air flowed inside the smoke alarms stopped.

"Mommy, mommy are you on fire again?" Karli asked as she stood in the kitchen carrying her favorite baby doll. She was rubbing her sleepy red eyes. The smoke alarms woke her.

"Oh no baby, mommy is fine. You see baby, I'm not on fire." I gave her a big hug. "Everything is fine, let me put you back to bed."

I carried Karli back to her bedroom to put her back to sleep. It didn't take long for Karli to fall back to sleep. She held onto my hand tightly. When I tried to leave her alone she wouldn't let my hand go.

"Mommy I don't want you to burn again. Can you please sleep with me so that I'll know you're safe?" Karli softly said.

Just when I was about to speak, Keith spoke instead. I didn't know that he was standing at the door. "Karli how would you like to sleep with your mom and me?" He smiled and asked her.

"I would really like that." Karli said.

I looked at the two of them back and forth. "Okay let me take a shower and change." I got up to take a shower.

It didn't take me but fifth teen minutes to shower and change. Tonight I put on my cotton top and bottom pajama set. Keith carried Karli into the room. We all got in my king sized bed. Keith slept closer to the door. I slept next to him and Karli slept under me. Damn I was horny tonight and ready to be fucked to sleep.

Chapter 5

Sunshine

The multiple hospital machines beeped nonstop. They were annoying the hell out of me. I reached for my clipboard of paper and pen. Writing everything down was my form of communication. On the paper I wrote down. *My head is hurting. I need something for pain. Have you spoken to my aunt?*

After I was done writing, I pressed the call light. Ten long minutes later, my dizzy nurse walked in. She turned off the beeping machines and apologized for their beeping. I handled her the clipboard so that she can read it. She took her time reading it, looked up and answered my questions.

"Yes you may have something for pain Melinda. I spoke to your aunt earlier. She said that she would be to visit you today. "The nurse replied.

She gave me something for pain intravenously. The pain medicine worked immediately causing my headache to diminish. I clicked a few buttons on my remote control until I found something worth watching on television. Cook County Hospital didn't have cable. I had to settle with watching the fucking Cosby Show.

"Alright Melinda is there anything else that I can do for you?" The nurse asked me.

I wrote down on the paper. "Please stop calling me Melinda. Please call me Sunshine."

She read the paper and apologized. "I'm sorry, I'll call you Sunshine from now on."

I rolled my eyes as I watched her leave out. Let me fill you in on why I hate to be called by my government name Melinda Carter. I'm named after my trifling mother. Yes I called her trifling because she's never been much of a mother to me. I was born July 19, 1990 right here in this very same hospital. Could you believe that I was born here and almost died here? Melinda pushed me out and resumed back to her daily habit. That was smoking crack. I was a crack baby and born prematurely. My aunt Marci took full custody of me from the first day that I left the hospital. I never got a chance to meet my father. He was gunned when my mom was six months pregnant with me. Before my mother started getting high she was beautiful. She met my father and started living the fast life. With the fast life came money, drugs and hate. Another drug dealer that my mother dated once upon a time, killed my father because he was envious that he was getting money and was with my mother. After my father was killed my mother started doing drugs heavily. Everyone who once loved Melinda loss all respect for her when she got strung out.

Growing up was cool except for the times that I was reminded of how much I resembled my crack head mother. My mother gave birth to me during the seventh month of her pregnancy. At the age of thirteen overnight I went from skinny to slim thick. My aunt Marci had a lot of sense by putting me on birth control when I started menstruating. In one year the Depo Provera caused me to gain weight making me thicker. The Chicago streets raised me, I was street illiterate. I hung out with a group of fast girls that were already fucking. It didn't take long for me to start having sex just like them. One day my friend told me how she got money and gifts from older boys every time that she had sex with them. From that point on any boy that I slept with had to take care of me. My nickname Sunshine came from my favorite movie, Harlem Nights. I fell in love with the character Sunshine and the way she had made Richie leave his wife. That's when I learned that pussy was very powerful. As I grew up I felt that I wasn't the relationship type of girl. Money was first love and what changed my life and circumstances. I became addicted to money and wanted more. That's when I hooked up with Tyrese and we both came up with a plan to make money. In the beginning Tyrese was one of my tricks. After several times of us having sex he came up with an idea of setting up niggas. I was down with idea as long as it was getting me more money. At first we were setting up niggas from out of Illinois. Hitting up Iowa, Wisconsin, Michigan, Ohio, New York and etc. The out of town jobs were easier to do because they didn't know me. Then Tyrese met Emani, fell in love and had children. It didn't stop us, instead I started setting niggas up locally.

When I begin getting up with Duke I was strictly about my money. As time went by, I started to fall in love with him. I was ready to put up my hoe card, marry him and have his children. The problem was that Duke never expressed how he felt for me until the night he was murdered. Now I have to live with his blood on my hands for the rest of my life.

The voice of the police officer that was guarding my hospital door caught my attention. I was moved and given security due to someone trying to smother me with a pillow. The hospital cameras caught a woman that was dressed in a scrub that entered my room and tried to kill me. When I heard about what happened, I knew who it was and who sent her. There was a tap on my hospital room door. In walked two men that were dressed and looked like detectives. I was preparing for this moment and knew why they were here. I'm from the streets and don't believe in snitching. When I get out of here I planned on handling this in another type of way. One of the detectives spoke first.

"Hello Melinda Ross, how are you today? I'm Detective Carr, your nurse said that it was fine if I asked you a couple of questions.

I took a look at the both of them and wrote down on my clipboard, *"Ask me questions about what?"*

He took a look at the clipboard reading it. "We have some leads that connect your shooting with Jabari Diggs and Tyrese Miller. Are you familiar with those two people?"

I shook my head no, taking advantage of not being able to talk.

"Miss Ross, I understand that you may not want to talk out of fear. I'm here to make a deal with you. You give us Tyrese Miller and you're free to go. Please keep in mind that you can be charged with Accessory facing ten years. If you cooperate the charge could be dropped."

Detective Carr remained quiet waiting on me to respond. Just in time, Aunt Marci walked inside my room. "Hello who are you?" She asked Detective Carr as she sized him up and down.

"Hello I'm Detective Carr, I'm here to talk to Melinda Ross and you are?" He extended his hand out for a handshake, but my Aunt Marci declined.

"I'm her Aunt Marcie, what's going on?" Marci was direct and straight to the point.

"I'm discussing the murder case of Duke? Miss Ross here could benefit a lot from what we discussed. I tell you what, I'll leave you my card and give you some time to think about what we discussed. Call me when you make a decision." He left his card leaving out with his partner following behind.

Aunt Marci rolled her eyes as she watched him walk out. She turned to look at me. "Sunshine I suggest that you do whatever you need to do to save your ass. Now I don't agree with snitching, but the son of a bitches turned on you. It's time that you think about yourself."

I started writing fast on my paper. "*I'm afraid that they would try to kill me again. I just want to get back better and relocate.*"

She read it while I was writing. "Don't worry about Bari, someone already killed him? Ty is the one that you need to be concerned about. But word on the street is that Ty is a wanted man. The same people that killed Bari is now on Ty ass." Marci told me.

I've been in the hospital trying to stay alive and didn't know any of this. "Say what, tell me more?" I wrote down.

"Word around town is that they fucked with the wrong niggas. They say that Emani set up some GD's from out south. It was a twin and Ty and Bari was behind it. Girl all types of mess. They ran Ty and Emani out of their own home. Nobody has seen them since." Aunt Marci told me.

Damn I didn't know all of this bullshit was going on. I do recall that someone tried to suffocate me while I was here.

The only people that wanted my ass dead was Ty. Instantly I prayed that Ty would get murdered just like Bari bitch ass did. Death would be a better choice because the last thing that I wanted to do was get on the stand to testify. They don't even know that I'm alive.

Chapter 6

Emani

Ty was foul for moving that old hoe into our home. Once again I was being weak by allowing him to control me again. Since the moment that I've been down with the plan, everything has been a disaster. Before all of this life was cool and my family was straight. Now I regret allowing Ty to talk me into setting up Jay. Crazy how things have changed. My baby boy Tyshawn was still in their possession. Tee was a man of his word and the clock is ticking. I swear if something happens to my baby boy, I'm done fucking with Ty! I'm so upset with him right now, we aren't on speaking terms. He hasn't slept in the bed with me ever since he has moved Tootie in. They both slept together in the room that Ty and I was supposed to share. My only concern at this moment was getting Tyshawn back home and running off with my children. Leaving Ty alone was the ultimate decision in my plans.

***

I locked myself inside my room from everyone. For the last couple of days I couldn't hold down anything that I ate. Drugs became my best friend, since I've loss the two that I had. The only person that I could trust was Big Momma. She was always a phone call away. My cellphone was powered off because I didn't want any interruptions. Due to everything that was going on my phone was ringing nonstop. People that I haven't heard from in forever was texting and calling me trying to be nosy. In reality they didn't give a fuck about me and wanted to know what they could spread to the next person. I decided to call my grandma. Her phone rang only once when she answered the call as if she was out of breathe.

"Hello Emani, Oh God I've been trying to reach you and Tyrese all morning. Please tell me that wasn't Tyshawn died body that they found?" Big Momma sounded worried on the other end of the phone.

I was puzzled and didn't know what she was talking about. "What boy? Who found what boy? Big Momma what are you talking about?" My heart started racing.

"It was on every news channel. A young boy body was found by the incinerator." Big Momma replied.

She was right, Big Momma always knew what was going on in the church and on the streets. She was that type of grandma that everyone confided in. When people needed advice or help they would stop by her house or give her a call. I searched for the remote control to my television so that I could find out what she was talking about. Turning on the television, I scanned for CLTV. The main story was a young boy body who was found with a shot wound to his chest. The description of the boy was Tyshawn's. Immediately I dropped my phone forgetting that Big Momma was on the line. In a rage I stormed down the hall to where Ty was resting his head. The room door was locked.

Bang! Bang! Bang! I banged on the mother fucking door so hard causing Lil Ty and Tyeisha to come out of their rooms.

"Mom what's going on?" They both looked at me strangely.

Ignoring my children I continued to bang on the door. Ty opened the door wearing only boxers. "Why in the fuck are you banging on the door for Emani?" he was mad that I woke his dumb ass up.

I rushed inside the room to see Tootie scrambling to put on one of his tee shirts. Fuck that hoe, I'll deal with her later.

"Ty is my son dead?! Don't bother to feed me anymore bullshit ass stories either!" Tears started flowing down my face.

"What are you talking about is Tyshawn dead? Where did you hear that from?" Right now Ty was displaying his lying face.

"Cut the bullshit Ty! What happened the other day? Tell me the truth for once and stop lying to me! What the fuck happened when you met up with Tavion?" I demanded to know.

The room was quiet as we all waited for Ty to reply. Ty had a look of sorrow in his eyes. Tootie broke the silence in the room, "Tell her, she deserves to hear the truth."

My eyes darted back and forth from Ty to Tootie and back onto Ty. "She know what's going on but I'm the only mother fucker that doesn't have a clue as to what's happening!" Ty backed me out of the room door trying to explain. I punched and kicked him, my tiny blows and kicks didn't faze him. Our children got in between us, separating the two of us.

"Ty how could you?! You're not shit and going to pay for every foul thing that you've ever did!" I stormed down the hall, Lil Ty and Tyeisha followed behind me. I picked my cellphone up from the floor, Big Momma was no longer on the line. Trying my best to calm down I called her back.

"Big Momma can you please contact the authorities and report that your grandson is missing and it's a possibility that he could be the young boy found by the incinerator."

"Oh God Emani, are you saying that Tyshawn is dead?" Big Momma replied.

"Can you please just identify the body and stop questioning me!" I raised my voice at her and ended the call. "**Fuck! Fuck! Fuck!**"

"Ma is our baby brother dead?" Lil Ty asked me.

I hugged and kissed them both softly on their forehead "I don't know babies, mommy doesn't know.

***

Two hours later I received the dreadful phone call from Big Momma confirming that Tyshawn was dead. One gunshot to his chest was what killed him. Ty basically killed our child himself even though he didn't pull the trigger. Big Momma told me that his body was found covered in a pile of trash. Right now I didn't want to live anymore, crying for God to take me out of my misery. Big Momma prayed for me on the phone until I stopped crying. She also informed me that the police was looking for me and Ty for questioning on Tyshawn's death and all the other events that occurred. I became nervous because they were going to connect the dots. First my home was shot up, second they found my son dead.

"Emani you and them children need to come back home now. Ty is going to get all of you killed as long as you're around him."

"Big Momma I can't go back there if I do they will try to kill me." I cried.

"Not if you go to the police and tell them that Ty made you do everything." Big Momma coached me.

Going to the police was out of the question. I live by the no snitching rule. Besides I wasn't innocent, knowing Ty he would drag me with him to prison. Ty and Tootie was better off died than alive. I'll deal with them when I cross that bridge. Right now I had to plan Tyshawn's funeral. With the help of Big Momma I told her everything to do. Although I wanted to take charge, I couldn't and had to stay afar.

"Big Momma I'm going to wire you some money under another name to handle Tyshawn's funeral expenses." She wrote down the alias name that I was using. I always kept multiple fake social security and identification cards.

After instructing Big Momma on what to do I called State Farm to start a claim. They gave their condolences and mailed the forms out to me to begin the process. I had all the paperwork sent to Big Momma's house because I didn't want the police to track me down. Big Momma would have to get his death certificate and do a number of things for me. The insurance policy that I had on all my children was a nice amount. It's fucked up that I'm burying my baby boy. He was the last one on mind when I thought about death. Ty was the first one that I thought would go first. I had a fifty thousand each on my children. I got dressed, throwing on a shirt and some leggings.

"Lil Ty I need you to get dressed and help your sister get dressed. We're about to make a run." I told them both.

"Yes momma." He walked off into their rooms.

Before leaving out I brushed my teeth. I looked and felt fucked up but I had to pull myself together. My two other children only had me because their father wasn't shit.

"Lil Ty!" I yelled for him as I brushed my teeth. He walked into the bathroom.

"Yes mom," he politely said.

"I need you to go and the car keys from your father."

Lil Ty walked off to get the keys. He was a spitting image of his father. However he was nothing like him. As a matter of fact none of my children were like their father, thank God for that. I gargled and rinsed with mouthwash, afterwards applied lip gloss to my lips. Ty gave up his keys without any drama. All three of us walked down the stairs and were headed out to the garage.

"Emani where are you going?" I looked back to see Ty standing at the top of the staircase. I rolled my eyes, ignored him and continued to proceed out of the door. "You better not do anything stupid like run off."

I gave Ty the middle finger. Left out and locked the door. A squirrel scared the living hell out of all three of us as it ran from behind the boxes that were in the garage. The boxes and duffel bag fell to the ground. Lil Ty and Tyeisha got inside the car as I walked over to see what was in the bag. It was heavy as I unzipped it. My eyes lit up as I ran my fingers across stacks of money. "*I'm about to take all this nigga money,*" I thought to myself. Damn this isn't the right time to do this. Instead I only took two stacks, totally twenty thousand. I smiled as I threw the money inside my purse. Ty wouldn't noticed if only two stacks were missing. I hid the duffel bag back behind the boxes. Ty had been holding out on me all this time. Getting inside the car I thought of ways that I could take off with the money. I didn't have any options, but I had to get out of this alive.

***

After sending the money off to Big Momma, the children and I went to our favorite place. TGIF was always conveniently right by our house. It wasn't crowded, therefore we were sat quickly. When the waiter came to the table take our orders I asked for two Pepsi's, a cocktail and three sizzling chicken skillets. Now was the time to have the talk with my children.

"Lil Ty and Tyeisha I have some bad news to tell the both of you."

"Momma we already know about our baby brother. Big Momma called us while you were in the bathroom. She told us to be strong for you." Lil Ty replied as he sipped on his Pepsi.

"I'm sorry about all of this craziness that's going on. I promise that everything will get better." I cried.

"Momma are you and daddy going to break up? Is that other woman our father new girlfriend? Why is she living with us?" Lil Ty spoke up, "We don't like her."

Not wanting to lose my temper inside of TGIF, I changed the subject back to Tyshawn's death.

"Tomorrow Big Momma is going to see about your baby brother funeral arrangements. It's a lot going on in the city preventing me to do such.

"Are we going to be able to attend the funeral? All of us as a family?" Lil Ty asked.

"Yes we will be there babies."

The waiter bought our sizzling chicken dinners to the table. *Damn how am I going to attend Tyshawn's funeral without getting killed?*

***

Today was Tyshawn's funeral. Tyrese was upset about me and the children attending. At this point I didn't give a fuck about the hit on me. I dressed up in disguise wearing a short blonde wig, black shades and all black. Nothing flashing or anything that resembled who I was. Tyeisha and Lil Ty was dressed in black as well. They sat in the rented Honda Accord waiting as me and their father argued.

"You're putting yourself and our children in danger. Are you crazy, are you fucking thinking?" Tyrese was big mad.

I stared cold into Tyrese eyes. "If I get popped or killed at my son's funeral so mutherfucking be it." Pulling up my top I revealed my bulletproof vest that I was wearing. "I'm good. I got this." My piece was on my hip with the safety on. They wasn't going to catch me slipping. Tyrese bitch ass allowed them to put fear in his heart.

We arrived to Corbin's funeral home. The local news stations was outside with their camera crew covering his story. Tyshawn's death was a big deal in Chicago. It was safer for me to park in the back, sliding through the back door.

"Alright you know the plan. Sit up front with Big Momma and I will sit in the back." I kissed the both of them. "I love you both. Please understand that I will be back to come and get you when everything dies down." I hugged them tightly.

"We love you too momma." They replied.

"Lil Ty and Tyeisha watch out for each other. Now go inside to kiss your baby brother goodbye."

They walked inside the funeral home. I waited ten minutes to go inside making sure not to cause any attention. There were a lot of people inside so it was easier for me to remain low key. Before entering Tyshawn's funeral recession I went to the bathroom. Luckily there wasn't anyone in there. There was no way that I was able to sit at my son's funeral without being high. The thoughts in my head told me, "*Just one hit Emani is all you need.*" I sniffed one toke quickly up my nose. This was some good shit. I rushed out before anyone walked in. An older woman handed me an obituary before I entered. Not wanting to be seen, I sat in the back. My family was deep in attendance. Some of Tyrese family was there too. "*Lord please don't let anyone notice me.*" It was two little small twin girls with their mom that sat in the same row as me. I scooted closer to them making seem as if we all were together. My black Christian Dior sunglasses hid majority of small face. I looked around to see who all was here. Tyshawn's teachers, social workers and a few of his classmates showed up. I was looking for a familiar face. I'm not surprised that Kamara didn't show up. She made herself clear that she wasn't fucking with me anymore. Big Momma's pastor started the service gaining everyone's attention. She also had two choir members sing. I watched from the back how she took it hard. My mother was by her side. She looked good, cleaned up nice for this day. A few of Tyrese family members were crying out loud putting on a show. *"Phony as hell"* His family never gave a fuck about us. Especially his mom, that bitch was as fake as a Made in China product. In order for me to keep my composure I needed some more nose candy. Sneakily, I sniffed some up my nose. The coke worked, taking me into a place of relaxation.

"In Matthew 19:14 But Jesus said, *"Let the little children come to me and do not hinder them, for to such belongs the kingdom of heaven."* The pastor said.

My children cried in Big Momma arms. I wished that I she could hold me too. I drifted off into another place. Everything around me begin to move in slow motion. I was feeling my high on another level. The funeral went on and it was time to view Tyshawn's body for the last time. Row after row people got up to give their last respect. *"Fuck it, I'm getting up to see my baby boy."* As I walked toward the front I kept my head down. My favorite cousin noticed it was me. We both locked eyes, quickly she yelled out crying and hollering.

"Why did my baby cousin have to die?" All of the attention was on her now.

Everyone watched as she cried and fell onto the floor. *"Thank you my favorite cousin,"* I said in my head. I stood only a moment at Tyshawn's casket before walking off fast and leaving. My baby didn't deserve this, it wasn't his time to go. If I could make one wish, I would ask for all of this to go away. Several people stood in the hall talking amongst themselves. I overheard two women with bad wigs talking major shit.

"What type of parents don't show up for their own child's funeral?" The one wearing a black tight dress with the gut replied.

"Girl I was waiting to see if they were coming because word around town is that they have a warrant out for their arrest." The tall, slim, manly looking one said.

"I hope that bougie bitch Emani does go to jail. I never liked her ass anyway." I was seconds away from snatching that hoe up until I heard gunshots outside."

"They shooting! They shooting!" someone yelled. Everyone started screaming, running and getting low. I took off out the back door in a hurry to the rental car. I didn't know who or where the gunshots came from directly. My hands trembled on the steering wheel as I sped down the alley. The shots continued. It sounded like a machine gun. My heart raced as I made it to Long Street. People ran in front of my car away from the gunfire. I blew my horn speeding off making a left turn. Never looking back, only ahead; I flew pass the stop sign. Sirens could be heard from afar.

Ring. Ring. Ring......My cellphone startled me, Tyrese number displayed across the screen. Harrison Avenue was clear, I rode it up to Central to jump on the expressway.

Ring….Ring…. "Hello," I replied as I wiped the snot from my nose.

"Where are you and my children? I just heard that Dee came through and wet up Corbin's." He yelled into my ear.

"Ty the children are safe with Big Momma. I'm on my way back to you right now."

"What do you mean that their with Big Momma? Emani you have to be the silliest bitch ever. Turn your ass around and go get my children!" he demanded.

"Ty fuck you! I'm not turning around to get them. I'm not going back, they cool with Big Momma." ***Click***!

The expressway was stop and go with so much damn traffic. Thoughts of turning myself in clouded my mind. That was risky, ain't no telling what they had on me. I had no choice other than to stay in this bullshit and keep on running. ***Ring…Ring…*** Big Momma was calling me this time. "Emani child are you fine?" I could hear the concern in her voice.

"Yes, how are you and the children? I got out of there as soon as I heard the gunfire."

"We're fine, however two of Tyrese cousins were shot. It's crazy up here, police are everywhere."

"Damn! Too bad for them. Are you on your way to the cemetery now?" I asked Big Momma.

"Yes but I don't think it's a good idea if you come to the burial. Emani go straight home and never come back this way again."

"Big Momma I don't plan to. Oh before I forget, Lil Ty has an envelope with cash for you. I'll send for Lil Ty and Tyeisha when things are safer."

"Don't worry about them, they'll be safe. I love you."

"I love you more Big Momma, call you tonight." **Click.** Tears ran down my face as I drove home.

***

Two hours later I arrived home. The house was clean however the weed greeted me at the door. I kicked off my shoes as I walked up the stairs slowly. The sounds of fucking came from the master bedroom. Tootie was screaming and moaning loudly as if Tyrese was killing her pussy. Tyrese didn't bother to close the bedroom door. Not giving a fuck I walked in interrupting their fuck session.

"Cut out all that fake ass yelling. I've been fucking him for several years and his dick ain't that damn amazing." Tyrese stopped drilling Tootie. He grabbed the sheet covering their bodies. "You didn't have the audacity to take a day off from fucking your whore on the day of your son funeral?" I threw his Polo boxers at him.

Tyrese got out of bed and slipped on his boxers. "Did anyone recognize you? Both of my cousins were shot. Lil Ryan and Byron were sent to Mount Sinai Hospital."

"As I was leaving the gunshots started. All the chaos was done in the front of the funeral home. Big Momma had it arranged for me to park in the back. A few family members noticed me and kept their cool."

Tyrese pulled a cigarette out of the box lighting it up. "This shit isn't going to never stop until I lay all of them mutherfuckers down. Any word on Tichina?" He asked as he sent smoke circles in the air.

"Nah, last thing I heard was that she's still alive. What's up with the plan that we discussed? When are we going to put this whore to work?" I was tired of the games, stalling and bullshit.

Tootie was in the process of rolling her a blunt, she paused giving both me and Tyrese a questionable look. Ty looked at me as if he wanted to smack the shit out of me.

"What the fuck is she talking about Ty? Please don't put me back out there in the streets, they will kill me." Tootie begged.

"I know that you didn't think that I was just allowing you to come inside my house, eat my food and fuck my man for nothing. Nah bitch, everything has a reason behind it. You use us and we use you. Now remove yourself out of my room, me and my man have something privately to discuss." I dared that bitch to talk back right now.

Tootie gathered her clothes and marched out of my room with her blunt in hand. Tyrese stared at her thick ass as it moved with the rest of her body. **Snap!** I snapped my fingers at him "Focus, you're allowing the ass to distracted you. We have to come up with a plan because Dee or Tavion aren't playing with us. The police have warrants out for our arrest. Right now I feel like we're boxed into a corner. We can only hide out here for so long."

"Emani I have a plan, chill out baby. If I can't get them one way, I'll get them another way." Tyrese had a sinister look on his face.

Chapter 7

Tichina

As I recovered from my shot wound Tavion and Kamara was by my side. I loss a significant amount of blood and had to receive a blood transfusion. My parents weren't too happy about that, however they prayed for me nonstop. It has been three weeks, the doctors finally removed the tubes and I was now on a clear liquid diet. My mouth was parched, I was weak and felt helpless. Today was my first day of physical therapy. Doctors' orders were for me to get out of the bed. Tavion and I were watching television when my bubbly physical therapist arrived pushing a wheel chair.

"Hello Tichina, how are you? I'm Natalie your assigned physical therapist. Today we are going to do a few therapy exercises. Are you up for the challenge?" She was cheerful and vibrant.

"Hi Natalie, I'm doing fine. I must admit that I'm a little nervous, but up to it." I gripped onto Tavion's hand as I spoke to her.

"Don't be nervous, I'm here to get you back walking. First, I want to help you sit in the wheel chair. Once we do we're going down to the physical therapy floor to have some fun."

"Sure, can my man come with me?" I asked Natalie.

"Yes of course he can."

Natalie raised me up in bed to a make it easier for me to sit in the wheel chair. With the help of Tavion, I was able to do that. I felt uncomfortable because of the urinary catheter that was inside of me. The three of us went the physical therapy floor. It was huge with a lot of equipment and other patients were there as well.

"Here we are Tichina. Today we're going to have you hold things and stand up." Natalie wheeled me over to a section with different objects.

The first thing that she had me to do was write. We threw a ball back and forth to each other. The good thing was that I was able to still do both. The hard part came when I had to stand. I was weak and afraid that I would fall. Tavion was by my side as I stood up for the first time.

"You can do it baby." Tavion encouraged me. I held onto the wooden beams and started to cry. "Can you give me a second alone with her?" Tavion asked the physical therapist.

"Sure, no problem." Natalie walked away to her desk giving me and Tavion some privacy.

"Tichina there is no reason to cry. I'm right here by your side to catch you when you fall. I love you beautiful, together we will get through this." Tavion kissed me on the forehead. He wiped away my tears and held my hands. "She's ready now Natalie."

Natalie came back over and we continued my hour physical therapy session. When we made it back to my room Kamara was there. I was so happy to see my best friend.

"Look at my best friend out of bed. Your nurse told me that you were having physical therapy and will be coming back soon. So I decided to sit here and wait for you. Hey Tavion, Keith is waiting outside for you." Kamara replied.

"What's up Kamara? Aye sweetheart I'll be back in a couple of hours. I'm going to handle some business. I love you baby." Tavion kissed me on the forehead.

"Be careful out there Tavion. I love you so much." I didn't want him to leave.

Tavion left and I became sad. My facial impression showed it all. Kamara tried to cheer me up. "Tichina I bought a handful of goodies in my bag. Today I'm going to give you two fish tail braids, apply a little makeup and fill you." Kamara happily said.

"First of all why is everyone so damn cherry today? Secondly, you're a bank teller not a makeup artist. You're not about to have me looking like a clown. Thirdly, girl spill all of the gossip. I've been so bored out of my mind. Tavion won't allow me to interact online. He doesn't think it's a good idea for me to be on social media." I dryly replied.

"He's right after everything that happened you should be out of sight. Let me start off with the sad news." Kamara reached inside her purse to pull out an obituary. "Wait let me get you some tissue because you're going to need it." She went into the bathroom to get me some tissue and closed my room door. "Here you go."

Kamara handed me both the obituary and piece of tissue. As I viewed the obituary I clutched my chest. A picture of Tyshawn's smiling face was on it. "No." I wept as tears fell from my eyes. At that moment I didn't want to open up to read the rest. Kamara hugged me as I cried. "That stupid selfish bitch of a mother of his." I angrily said.

"It was hard for me not to say goodbye to him. Emani and Ty is still on the run. Some bitch named Tootie too is on the run. They shot up the funeral and everything. This shit has gotten out of hand. I'm afraid and can't sleep at night. Keith has been with me and Karlie 24/7. Tichina I'm walking around here with a bullet proof vest on and two pieces on me." Kamara showed me her vest along with her gun on her waist. After that she showed me her second piece that was inside her purse.

"I can't believe that Tyshawn had to die for his parents actions. Where is Lil Ty and Tyeisha?" I asked Kamara.

"Keith got a call the other day, the caller said that they were at Big Momma's house. Don't worry about them. Tavion didn't approve for them to get harmed. They had to calm Dee down before he went on a killing rampage."

"You know what's crazy? After everything that Emani has put me through I actually forgive her." I dryly replied.

"Fuck that bitch and that hoe ass nigga of hers. She better hope that I don't catch up with her ass. Emani has been cut throat for a long time. This time around she pulled the bullshit on us. I wished that we would've got rid of them both earlier on." Kamara angrily said.

"Kamara I should've listened to you when you tried to warn me."

"Tichina you were just being a friend and gave her the benefit of the doubt. When Tavion came in your life he became your main focus. He had all your attention, so you didn't pay attention to anything else going on around you."

"What's crazy is that Emani and Tyrese thought that they were going to get away with it. All of time she continued to smile in my face and was plotting against me." I shook my head.

"That's what dirty hoes from the Chi do. We just never thought that our friend was one of them dirty hoes." Kamara replied.

We chatted as Kamara washed and French braided my hair. It was the best hairstyle but it was better than my hair being all over my head. Kamara has always been real and upfront about everything. With her you never had to second guess or think twice. Emani was always extra and an attention whore. When we were younger her attitude was terrible to deal with. That's why she didn't have many friends. Kamara and I felt that she had a bad attitude because of the way her mom was. We excused that and became three besties. As the years went by Emani became softer when she had her children. At times that rude bitch would appear whenever she and Tyrese were feuding. Emani said that she was going to leave him countless of times. The more money that Tyrese brought in, Emani wasn't going anywhere. We both knew that Tyrese lifestyle would catch up with him and Emani. Never in a million years had I thought that she would turn against me.

Hours went by and I was starting to become sleepy. Kamara didn't want to leave me alone until Tavion came back to the hospital. She gave me a bed bath as I laid in bed. I cried as she washed me up.

"Kamara thank you so much." I cried.

"Tichina don't cry, you know that I got your back. I love you and will do whatever it takes to get you back on your feet. We've been friends since we were playing double-dutch and hop scotch with pig tails. You don't have to thank me for anything."

We hugged one another, that's when Tavion walked into the room smiling. He startled Kamara and me because we didn't hear him enter.

"What's up beautiful, I see that Kamara hooked you up on the hair side." Tavion smiled and said.

Kamara got up to empty the water out of the wash basin. She prepared to leave and gathered her things. "Is Keith waiting down stairs for me?" She asked Tavion.

Knock...Knock... "Come in." Tavion said.

Kamara and I looked at each other. Keith walked into the room smiling surprising me.

"Keith is that you?" I happily asked him. This was Keith's first time coming to visit me while I was in the hospital.

"How are you doing sis? I'm sorry that I haven't been up here to see you." He hugged me softly.

"I'm doing much better, started physical therapy today." I replied.

"You looking good. Really good, if you need anything I'm a phone call away." Keith hugged Kamara, grabbing her butt.

"Thank you Keith and you too are something else. You got my girl sprung, she talked my ear off about you. Keith this, Keith that." We all laughed.

"Tichina I'm not telling you anything else." Kamara giggled like a young teenager.

I was happy to see my best friend back in love again. There was nothing like loving somebody and somebody loving you back. They left leaving Tavion and I alone. Tavion smelled and looked good.

"How was your day today?" I asked him.

"It almost got a little crazy. We had to have a long talk with Dee, sit him down and tell him to chill the fuck out. His ass will have us all in jail for bodies and I'm not going out like that." Tavion became slightly upset.

"How did that go? You know losing a brother is hard especially when it's your twin. I feel so bad for him." I replied.

"You know how Dee is, it took some time to calm his ass down. We explained to him that we didn't have any room for error. Everything will get taken care of. If he continues to go on a killing rampage things could get out of hand."

"I agree with you, like the killing of my god son."

Tavion looked over at me with regret in his eyes. "I'm so sorry that he was killed. That wasn't planned, Tichina his pussy ass father used him for a fucking shield."

"Why am I not surprised to hear that? Tyrese is that type of fucked up person. I'm surprised that Emani will even allow him to get inside her head." I said.

"Fucked up bitch was smiling in your face during the day. At night she was pillowing talking with her nigga. That's okay because I swear to God that they both getting what's coming to them."

Tavion and I changed the subject into something lighter. He didn't want me to get upset or deal with the situation. Deep down inside I feared for Emani right now. She's not that bright and will get caught slipping soon.

Chapter 8

Tootie

Things were all changed here at Tyrese house. Tichina worked her magic back into her man turning him against me. Damn I was so very close to getting rid of her. Well at least I thought I was until I see that she returned back without her children. This fucking bitch had the nerve to start bossing me around like she was in charge. Tyrese agreed to whatever she said. It was like she had him hanging by the balls. I was no longer in the bedroom with him. I slept in the guest room down the hall. Now I was enduring the sounds of him and Emani fucking at all times over the house. What was I to do? Where could I go without any money? I was stuck here, alone spending most of my time in the room watching television. The only person who I could talk to was my friend Bridget. I no longer felt comfortable or trusted Tyrese. I never trusted or fucked with Emani. It was after seven pm. Bridget should be home from work by now. Calling her was the last thing that I wanted to do. We always had our ups and downs, but that still was my girl. I needed someone to know what was going on just in case some foul shit went down.

I called Bridget privately blocking my number. She didn't need to know my number in order for me to talk to her. She answered the call on the fourth ring.

"Hello." Bridget answered sounding as if she was sleeping.

"Hey Bridget wake up this is me, Tootie." I replied.

"Oh my God, Tootie bitch where in the fuck have you been?" Bridget woke up from out of her sleep.

"Girl I'm tucked off away. Far, far away." I couldn't complete my sentence without Bridget cutting me off from talking.

"Your family have been looking for you. Questioning and interrogating the fuck out of me as if I was lying about not knowing your whereabouts."

I looked over my shoulder making sure the bedroom door was locked. "I'm with Tyrese and Emani hiding out." I whispered into my cellphone.

"What? Where? How did you end up with the both of them? I mean I knew that you were hiding out, but I never thought that you would end up with them." Bridget dryly said.

"What else was I supposed to do Bridget? I didn't have any money or know other place to go. Look I don't need you to be judging me right now. This is why I didn't want to call you in the first place."

"Wait, please don't get upset with me. I'm here for you and on your side. Where are you?" Bridget asked me again.

"I'm safe that's all that you need to know." I spoke lowly.

"You don't sound like it. Tootie what's going on? You reached out to me now for a reason."

"Okay the reason why I reached out to you was to tell you who I was with. Just in case if you don't hear from me then you would know who I'm with."

"Tootie are you being held captive by them? Just be honest with me, tell me what the fuck is going on?"

"Bridget I'm telling you more than enough already damn! You know what, I should've not called you. Tell my parents that I love them and that I'm doing fine. Good bye Bridget."

"Nooooo, please don't hang up the phone. We can't end our phone call like this. Tootie are you there?" Bridget took a look at her phone screen. The call was still active.

"I'm still here, afraid, alone. I don't know what to do. I don't know what their up to. Have you been hearing anything in the streets about me?" I cried into the phone.

"It has to be something that you can do. What happened to all the cash that you were telling me that Tyrese had. Hell what happened to the money that you said you made working with him? The streets are talking, their looking for the three of you. Tootie I told you not to get involved with Tyrese and his bullshit."

"I only have about five thousand to my name. That's not enough money to start over with. I need to get my hands on some more money. I know that Tyrese has some money around this big house of his."

"Big house? What you mean by big house?" Bridget curiously asked me.

"Tyrese had a home away from home that no one knew about. We're all here hiding. I don't trust them at this point but I don't have anyone else to help me. It's not all that bad though. I just have to do whatever they tell me to do." I replied.

"I'm confused, do you go out the house at all? Do you think that you could get some type of job and get your own place? With five thousand dollars that should be enough for one month's rent and security." Bridget was thinking short term.

"Bridget I can't start over with that small about of money. Besides I'm trying to get out of Illinois. If I want to stay alive I have to leave this fucking place. Wait hold on Bridget I think that I hear someone coming up the stairs." I placed Bridget on hold as I walked to my bedroom door to take a peep out of it. The sound of Tyrese's voice echoed in the hall, he was on his way upstairs. "I have to go Bridget bye." **CLICK**

I hurried up to lay across my bed as if I was watching the movie that was playing on the fifty inch flat screen. Tyrese tapped on my bedroom door. I turned my head to see what he wanted. He had a look of lust in his eyes. In my mind I wanted him badly. Instead I rolled my eyes, acting as if I was upset with him.

Tyrese sat on the end of the bed. "What's up, what are you watching on television." He smacked my ass.

"Don't touch me nigga. You have some damn nerves. Trading up on me and shit. You foul Tyrese, you mother fucking foul."

"Tootie what do you expect for me to do. Emani is wifey, whatever she says goes. You knew this from the jump. If I was foul your ass would be out there trying to survive on your own." Tyrese rubbed my thighs as he tried to explain the bullshit.

"What was Emani talking about? So you two have plans for me? What type of plans Tyrese?" I turned around to look into his eyes. Tyrese smiled and licked his lips.

"I was thinking that we could keep the business going. Instead of hooking up with drug dealers, we can target wealthy white men."

"Tyrese I don't know about that, you're not about to put me out there like that. How much money do you plan on making?" I was livid.

"It's not only going to be you, Emani is going to work with you as well. She's going to set you up on a dating site where white man are looking exclusively for black women. I heard about this site a long time ago and had plans on doing that next with some new girls. We can make plenty of money Tootie." Tyrese rubbed the side of my right cheek.

"Tyrese what's my cut?" I smacked his hand down from my face.

"We're splitting everything down the middle 50/50 baby."

"50/50, how about 70/30? You're not doing nothing but collecting the money. Tyrese we're on another level. I need a pay raise, besides you're not out there risking your life."

"Tootie baby that's where you're wrong at. I'll be on security with every move. I'm risking my life too. Now I'll cut you some slack on the pay increase. 60/40 that's what I can do thickness. Just keep it between me and you." Tyrese kissed me softly. "I miss every inch of you Tootie."

I gripped Tyrese dick. "I miss every inch of your dick." I looked at the doorway.

"Emani went to Popeye's to buy some chicken. We have about twenty minutes to ourselves."

Keeping his clothes on Tyrese unzipped his pants and pulled out his dick threw the hole in his boxers. I slurped on his dick until he came inside my mouth. Tyrese pulled his pants up quickly as I spat his nut out into the plastic bag that was hanging on the door knob. He went back down stairs and waited for Emani to walk thru the door.

Ten minutes later I heard Emani walk through. Tyrese called me to come down to join them. We played it off as if I just didn't get finished sucking his dick. Emani took a look at me with a smirk on her face; as if she knew that Tyrese and I had been up to something. She made sure that she took all the best pieces of the chicken. Leaving me and Tyrese the dry ass breast. All three of us sat at the large dining room table eating. Tyrese broke the silence bringing up our next move. I acted as if this was my first time hearing what our next lick was. As Tyrese explained everything he stated that we would split everything 50/50. Emani was surprised that I was down for everything so easily.

"I'm surprised that you're so down with all of this." Emani said as she used her hands to talk.

"Why is that? When have I not ever been down with anything that Tyrese ask me to do? You on the other hand is the person that's always a Debbie downer." I smiled as I got up to leave from the table but Tyrese grabbed my arm.

"Wait I'm not finished yet, tonight I'm setting up your profiles. I want to get things done ASAP. Time to get money rolling back in until I can get somethings started." He said.

"Got cha, I'm ready whenever you're ready." Tyrese and I locked eyes.

Emani sat back watching our body language. The look in her eyes told me that she didn't seem comfortable with what she was witnessing. That was my cue to leave. Removing myself from the dining room I went back to my room. That was the first time that I felt something strange about Emani. Her silence made me nervous. The bitch was up to something, now I had to be on my toes. I was afraid and haven't been afraid in such a very long time. Before I went to bed I said a prayer.

Dear God please cover me now more than ever. I know that I've did some awful things to many people. I'm asking you for forgiveness. I'm tired of living this lifestyle. I pray that you deliver me from this ugly person that I've been for such a long time, Amen.

After I was done praying I laid down to get some rest. At this moment it was really about survival. I was running from the enemy and living with enemy. No one could be trusted. My next mission was to stack my bread and get ghost on Tyrese ass. If I had to sleep with one eye open as long as I lived here, well so be it.

Chapter 9

Emani

Tyrese and Tootie must think that I'm dumb as Forrest Gump. As I watched the two get cozy with their eyes right in front me. Their body language showed that they fucked while I made my food run. At this point I didn't give a fuck and knew that they did. You know that I know not to trust Tyrese anymore. Last week I sat up a camera in my home that allowed me to view my house on my phone. I watched Tyrese ease upstairs to Tootie. I laughed as I was her sucked my man dick threw his boxer hole. I played it off with silence. That's right no more turning up on Tyrese or the fighting. I was trying to make a major move without his ass. Playing his game as long as I stacked enough bread to leave his ass. If selling my pussy was my only option to get out of this jam. I was going to pop this pussy on every white men's dick. Tyrese and I went upstairs to our master bedroom to get things started. He sat up an account on a popular dating website that frequently looked for escorts. This website wasn't your ordinary Back Page or Tinder bullshit. This was a top of the line dating website where wealthy white men who loved to get spanked with paddles shopped on. He set up a profile that described me and Tootie like we were houses for sell. If any man wanted us, step two was to set up a private conservation in our chat room. From there they would see our pictures and if they were pleased with us we will set up a date. Once that was set up Tyrese and I fucked before I put his ass to sleep.

***

It was 9:13 am when I opened my eyes. Tyrese wasn't lying next to me, he was already up. I could hear music playing from our bathroom. He was inside shaving the hair off his face.

"Good morning beautiful. You were sleeping so beautifully that I didn't want to wake you." He happily sang the song on the radio that I didn't know.

"Aren't we so cherry this morning?" I sat on the toilet to pee. Tyrese kissed me on the cheek before he left out of the bathroom to sit on the bed.

He grabbed the laptop and scanned the web. I wiped my ass, flushed the toilet and washed my hands. Tyrese talked about something but I couldn't barley hear him from the music and water running. I grabbed my toothbrush, toothpaste and began to brush. Whatever artist that was singing on the radio couldn't sing at all. I turned the music off so that I could hear Tyrese better. He was baffling on and on about whatever he was viewing on the web. I and my minty breath joined him plopping down next to him. He was on the exclusive dating website checking out our potential clients.

"Baby we received a lot of requests from you and Tootie's post last night." He was happy, all he seen was dollar signs."

"Let me check it out." Taking over the laptop that was in Tyrese hands. There was several men requesting our services.

I breezed through the comments that they sent. Some of them didn't require much. Some sent pictures of themselves. Then you had those that were straight to the point about fucking and having fun. I couldn't believe how much white men loved them some dark meat.

"So what's next?" I questioned Tyrese.

"Next is setting you two up. It's totally your choice on who you want to be with and what you want to do." He said.

"That's cool, I'm down for whatever. What's going on back home with your other girls, Sweetie and Tweety? Are they still doing their thing with you or you just dumped them?" Shit I wanted to know what the fuck was going on.

"Maine is taking over and running things back there in Chicago. I'm done with Sweetie and Tweety slow asses." Just like that, Tyrese was done fucking with them and left them behind.

I stared at him, he read my eyes. Tyrese was a cold person right now I didn't know if he was telling the truth or lying.

"Tyrese I'm not doing this shit for long. One month is all I'm down for. With the money we have, the money we make and putting this house on sell. We should be able to start all over somewhere else."

"Emani baby I got you and going to take care of you and our children forever." He kissed me on my right cheek. "After this we should be cool, I have some connects down south in Georgia. We can start all over there and live comfortably."

"Georgia? Everyone from Chicago always run down to Georgia. That's a mini Chicago, trust me we won't be able to live there in secrecy. We have to relocate somewhere low-key if you want to stay alive."

Tyrese wasn't thinking with a damn full deck right now. He was never able to think straight when he was under pressure. I was always the brains in the relationship. The one time that I slipped up and allowed him to run shit look what happened. This time around I wasn't allowing him to blow it. Although I didn't want to sell pussy I had to do something. I continued to check out the potential clients. Tyrese called Tootie into the room with us. She came inside with a smile on her face. That bitch was being too damn cheerful around here. I had to keep my eye on her, she was up to something. Tootie and I went through the request that we received. Thirty minutes later we made plans to hook up with three men a piece tonight at various locations out here. What they wanted was easy, it was best if we started off slow instead of moving too fast. My first client was meeting with me at 6pm. Tootie had a client at 7pm. We both had several clients after. The scheduling was off and there was no way that Tyrese was able to be at two places at one time.

"Tyrese how are we going to this? You said that you were security. With the scheduling it's impossible for you to be with me and with her." I asked him.

Tootie and Tyrese both took a look at each other. "I'm good being by myself. Just give me a gun for protection. Fuck them, get paid and go. It's that simple." Tootie replied.

"Alright check this out, you both will be strapped. If a person give you a problem do what you have to do. No exceptions, you feel me." Tyrese told us.

I shook my head up and down. Honestly I didn't want to add on anymore situations to my problems. Tyrese stared at me as Tootie continued to flap her mouth about something. He could feel that I felt uneasy about doing this.

"Tootie why don't you take a look at your client profiles, get a feel of them. So that you would know what to expect tonight. While you're doing that pick out something nice to wear too." Tootie took the laptop from Tyrese walking off to her room.

Tyrese rubbed my shoulders massaging them trying to make me feel comfortable. The massage felt good but it didn't stop my nervousness.

"Emani baby please don't get nervous on me now. I need you more than ever so that we could get out this jam and shake this bitch."

"What if this shit doesn't go as planned like all your ideas don't. You saying have a gun on you as if that shit solves anything. Ty don't you think that we're already knee deep in bullshit as it is?"

"Look one month is all we need Emani baby. I promise after this I'm done with all the setting up niggas, robbing, selling pussy and all." He hugged me from behind and kissed the side of neck. My nipples hardened and my clit jumped as he kissed my hotspot.

"Stop, you know what you're doing." I giggled pushing him off of me. "I'm just a little nervous about being with a white a man." I turned to look at him.

"That's understandable. If it helps thinking about me while you're sleeping with them, then do so. Emani think about all the money that you're about to make. These aren't your ordinary white men, these are wealthy white men."

"This is the last time Ty, you understand me?!" I playfully punched him the chest. He fell down on the California King sized bed laughing.

"Alright, now go pick something sexy out tonight to wear. Let me continue setting up your appointments."

Tyrese went to go handle hoe business as I searched for the sexiest pieces to wear tonight. Not having many to choose from I decided to wear red from head to toe. I picked out a red sexy lingerie set as well. I took a look in the mirror as I held the pieces up to my body. I thought to myself, *I'm going to be a hot little red corvette tonight.*

Chapter 10

Tootie

I was bent over in the closet going through the shoe boxes when Tyrese came up behind me. He playfully pumped me from the back. Laughing I picked out some black heels to try on. Tyrese was excited about all of this. I on the other hand wasn't as excited. Getting money was the only thing on my mind. Every dollar added up at this point. As I stood up to step in my shoes Tyrese took a seat on the edge of the bed scanning on the laptop.

"You had a talk with the First Lady?" I jokily said, not giving a damn if she was cool with it or not.

"Yeah we good to go." Tyrese rubbed his chin as he looked at the screen. "Aye you are cool with taking an Uber to and from your places?" He asked me.

"Sure as long as it's not coming out of my pay."

"Nah, I'll set up an account and take care of that for you. Tootie it won't be all the time that you would have to take an Uber. There will be some times when the schedule may not conflict with Emani's."

"Cool with me. I'm just ready to make this money."

I mixed and matched several pieces of clothes and shoes together. When of my clients requested to see me in all black. The other two clients didn't wasn't picky. I've slept with other men outside of my race before, but not a white one. They all were the same when it came to the color green. One of my clients was kindly enough to send me a nude picture of him holding his dick. I'm pleased to say that all white men aren't as small as what I heard. That amped my pussy up, I replied back quickly to him saying that I can't wait to bounce on that mother fucker. One thing about me is that I loved to fuck. Besides Tyrese wasn't dicking me down on a regular thanks to his hating ass bitch. I had an itch that needed to be scratched.

It was now show time, Tyrese gave Emani and I each a gun for protection. I was more than ready to pop this pussy and make some money. Emani seemed calmer than earlier, being nice to me and shit. Even though I didn't fuck with her I played along. We were both dressed nicely I must say. I was wearing a simple one shoulder black dress with a pair of black sling back heels. My makeup was flawless, with a purple lip to add color. My black straight weave flowed down my back as I rocked 20 inches. Emani had on a red bandage dress, a pair of red four inch heels making her appear taller. She looked like a video vixen with her cute shape. She wore a blunt cut bob wig. Very little makeup with a red lip. We were both going to fulfill a white man's dream tonight. Tyrese went over everything with us again. I ordered my Uber, twelve minutes my driver arrived taking me to my distention.

Upon arriving to my clients house I texted him to let him know that I arrived. The driver drove through the black gates down the long driveway. Before stepping out I made sure that I was perfect. I took one last glance in the mirror to check my hair, face and teeth. The Uber driver smiled and told me to have a nice day. My black sling back heels tapped on the cobblestone as I walked up the stairs to ring the bell. A black woman opened the door. She was dressed as if she was his maid. I wanted to tell her that we were free now. However from the looks of things I could tell that she was getting paid a nice amount.

She greeted me, "Hello Miss Tootie, Mr. Dunbar is waiting for you in the master bedroom upstairs."

"Thank you." I politely said as I followed her to the elevator.

Damn, Mr. Dunbar was living, he was the one with the big dick that I was anxious to ride. I got on the elevator, got off and stood in front of his door. Before I could knock he told me to enter. I figured that he watched me from the cameras in his home. I entered, Mr. Dunbar was a very attractive older man. Tall, with dark brown hair, nice teeth and muscles. He smiled when he seen me.

"You're beautiful, perfect just like your pictures." He said as he walked around me viewing my body as if I was a car. "Take your clothes off, get comfortable." Mr. Dunbar requested.

He poured us a glass of champagne while I undressed. I laid across his bed wearing only my black bra and thong. Mr. Dunbar eyes scanned my body up and down. He handed me the bubbly champagne. I took one sip slowly not wanting to gulp it down all at once. He joined me in his enormous bed wearing only his satin black boxers. I took the initiative to speak first.

"I've never done this before, honestly you're my first client." I nervously said.

He stared into my eyes. "I've done this plenty of times and I must say that you're one the beautifulness of them all."

I blushed, "Is that so? You probably tell that to all of your women." I grabbed his dick which was brick hard.

"No I don't. Tootie tell me about yourself. I'll like to get to know more about you."

"You don't want to get started? You do know that we only have an hour." I told Mr. Dunbar.

"Yes I'm aware that you'll be accompanying me for an hour," he flashed his pearly perfect white teeth.

Mr. Dunbar poured me more champagne. I told him what I wanted him to know without getting to personal. He shared a few things about himself as well. He was 55, an owner of ten apartment complexes who loves to work out and was married. His late wife was black and died of breast cancer two years ago. He was married for twenty one years. Had one son who died at the age of nineteen in a car crash. As I listened to Mr. Dunbar tell me about his life I felt bad for him. He had all this money and didn't have anyone left in his life to share it with. Now usually I wouldn't believe a person who I just met. Something in Mr. Dunbar eyes told me that he was telling the truth. Before I knew it an hour had passed. We both talked and laughed about everything. There was no fucking or getting intimate involved.

"Mr. Dunbar, I hate for this to end but my hour is up." I proceeded to get dressed.

Mr. Dunbar rubbed my hands softly. "Do you mind staying with me for another hour? I have money to pay you whatever the price is."

"I'm sorry but I have other plans."

"I see, Miss Tootie." Mr. Dunbar watched me get dressed.

He handed me a white enveloped filled with money as I ordered my Uber. To my surprised he walked me out. I didn't want to leave, but something tells me that this won't be the last time that I see Mr. Dunbar. My car arrived.

We both gazed into each other eyes. "Goodbye Mr. Dunbar."

"Not goodbye, see you soon Miss Tootie." He said.

"Yes see you soon Mr. Dunbar." I smiled and got inside the car.

As the driver drove away I looked at Mr. Dunbar as he walked back into his big empty home. I counted the money in the enveloped. It was an extra three hundred dollars inside. I slid that money in my bra. Right on time, Tyrese called to check on me. I answered telling him that everything was running smoothly as planned. Tyrese will never know about what happened or the extra money. My first job was easier than I thought that it would be. Now on to my next client which was dinner and playtime afterwards. After that I had another late night client that I had to meet at a hotel.

Six hours later I was exhausted and tired from eating good, drinking and all the fucking that I was doing. I made an extra seven hundred dollars in tips combined from all three of my clients. Tyrese and Emani waiting for me in front of the hotel. She was already done for the day with her clients. I got inside the car we both talked briefly about our first experience. When we made it home I paid Tyrese, soaked in some hot water and dragged myself to bed. In the morning I woke up to a smiling Tyrese in my face.

I jumped up, "Why are you smiling in my face like that?! You scared the fuck out of me!" I said.

"Tootie I don't know what you did yesterday with Mr. Dunbar. He requested to see you today for six hours." Tyrese happily said.

"What are you serious?" My heart skipped a beat or two.

While Tyrese counted dollars I thought deeper than that. Mr. Dunbar had to like me just as I much as I liked him. I certainly felt a connection with him that was hard to resist. Today good be the start of something new for me if I played my cards right.

Chapter 11

Dee

Maine jumped out of the freshly cleaned Lexus that he just had copped. He entered the back door of the trap house. When he stepped inside the house was quiet.

"Sweety! Tweety!" He yelled both of their names. He took a cold Pepsi out of the fridge and popped it open. "Where the fuck are these hoes at" Maine proceeded to walk in the front room.

There he found both Sweety and Tweety tied up to chairs. Dee and Keith were sitting on the couch with their guns pointed at them.

"What the fuck!" Maine dropped his Pepsi and tried to run out the back door.

Pop! Dee shot him in the leg. Sweety and Tweety cried as they witness Maine going down. Dee dragged Maine by the arm back into the living room.

"You already know why we're here. Where is Tyrese and his bitch Tootie at?" Dee asked him.

Maine held onto his wounded leg. "Man I don't know where they fuck them at. When you find out let me know because that nigga owe me some money." Maine angrily said.

Dee laughed wickedly, "Wrong answer I suggest that you think long and hard before you answer me again." He cocked his gun.

"You might as well kill me because I'm not telling you shit!" Maine spat.

POW! Dee sent one shot through his head. Maine head hit the hardwood floors as blood rolled out of his head.

Sweetie and Tweety whimpered as they watched Keith and Dee aim their guns to their heads. ***POW! POW!*** Both of their heads fell forward. Keith and Dee walked out the side entrance of the raggedy trap house. Dee felt a little better because the leads were getting him closer to his targets. They jumped in the Cadillac truck and sped off.

"We going to find them mutherfuckers!" Dee commented. Right before his phone his rang. It was his woman Dasia calling him. "What's up bae?" He calmly answered.

"Dee where are you? My water just broke, I'm on my way to the hospital now." Dasia cried.

"Bro, Dasia is in labor her water broke. We have to meet her at UIC hospital now." Dee anxiously said.

Keith punched on the brakes speeding down the street. He ran stop signs until he made it to the expressway. Dee watched out for the police so that they didn't get pulled over. They made it to UIC emergency room. Dee ran out of the car while Keith went to park. The emergency room was busy with many people sitting around. There was a long line at the receptionist desk. Dee wasn't feeling that long, rudely cutting off the seven people in front of him. They all yelled and cursed him out.

Dee ignored them addressing the nurse that was sitting behind the desk. "Excuse me, I'm looking for a black pregnant woman that came in her not too long ago."

"What's the name of the patient?" The nurse asked him.

"Dasia Walker." He frantically said. The nurse tapped on the keyboard searching to see if they have a patient by that name.

She looked up, "Yes she just arrived and has been rushed up to Labor and Delivery. Sir may I ask who you are?"

"I'm Dustin her man, the father of our unborn children." He calmly spoke.

"Dustin I need identification in order for you to go up." Dee pulled out his wallet presenting his license to the nurse. She registered him into the system on the computer. After she was done, Dee was given a name tag and visitor pass to go upstairs. "You can go down the hall, make a right and the elevators will be straight head. Labor and Delivery is on the fifth floor." The nurse instructed him.

Dee rushed off toward the elevators. Dasia wasn't expected to have the twins for another seven weeks. He panicked while bad thoughts filled in his head. The elevator took him to the fifth floor where she was at. Dee checked in but wasn't allowed to go inside. Dasia had to have an emergency cesarean section. Dee took a seat in the waiting area. He was afraid that he may lose his twins. Keith walked in, he saw the look of failure on his childhood friend face.

"Are Dasia and the twin's fine?" Keith asked him.

"They're performing a cesarean section on her now. Keith you know that Dasia isn't due yet, what if my twins don't make it." Dee shamefully implied.

"Why would you think negatively right now? Its millions of premature babies born that live and grow up to be perfectly healthy. You're talking to one of them right now." Keith told Dee.

"Damn bro I didn't know that, why haven't you never told us?" Dee asked Keith.

Dee his twin brother Jay, Tavion and Keith all grew up together since they were younger. Not one time did Keith mention that he was a preemie?

"I don't know why I didn't tell yall. That doesn't matter right now. What matters is that you remain positive and strong. Dasia and the twins will be fine. Stop blaming yourself for this. Carrying twins are a lot of a woman's body. Therefore her risks are higher while she's pregnant."

Dee sat there taking in all the knowledge that Keith was throwing at him. He thought about his twin brother Jay and wished that he was here by his side. He missed his brother dearly and felt that his death caused him to act out irrational at times. Dasia was the only person that could keep him calm. That's why he blamed himself for Dasia's early labor. Dee's actions were stressing Dasia out. Dee snapped out of the trance when the operating nurse walked up to them.

"Hello which one of you are Dustin?" The nurse was dressed up as if she just left out of surgery.

"I'm Dustin." A nervously Dee stood up and said.

The nurse smiled as she looked at Dee and announced. "Congratulations you're the father of two twin baby girls. By Dasia having them earlier in her third trimester they weighed only four pounds each." The nurse noticed the concerned look upon Dee's face. "Please don't be scared or nervous. Your babies are now in our neonatal intensive care unit getting monitored. If this would put a smile on your face, Dasia is ready to see." The nurse smiled at Dee.

Dee anxiously wanted to see Dasia and his babies. He and Keith both followed the nurse to where Dasia was. Seeing Dasia laid in the hospital bed made his heart soften up. He no longer was that hard person who just killed three people an hour ago. Dee gave Dasia a big hug and a forehead kiss.

"I love you baby so much. I promise to be the best father to our twin girls." Dee cried softly.

Dasia looked into his eyes and started to cry. "I love you too. Now you have two baby girls who are depending on you to be here for them." She was stern with her comment.

Dee knew what she was talking about. Yesterday Dasia had a long talk with him about his menacing behavior. She opened up her heart by telling him how much she and twins needed him in their lives. Keith stood afar while waiting for Dee to finish embracing his woman. Watching the both of them made him think about Kamara and her beautiful daughter Karlie. He loved Kamara and took the time to pull out his phone to send her a simple *'I love you,'* text message. Kamara responding back quickly with *'I love you',* back and blowing kisses emoji's.

"Hey Keith come over here and give me a hug." Dasia called out to Keith.

Keith smiled as he walked over to her. "Congratulations sister and don't worry I'll make sure to keep Dee in check for you."

Dasia and Dee both chuckled. "Ouch!" Dasia grabbed her stomach where they cut and stitched her back up at. She was wearing a white waist band around her stomach.

"Is everything fine? Do you need me to go and get the doctor?" Dee panicked.

"No doctor needed honey. Everything is fine, for a second I forget about my c section until I laughed. Dasia pressed the button of the IV drip that was flowing through her veins to stop her pain.

"Would you like to know your daughters names? Dasia smiled at Dee.

He grabbed her hand. "Yes I would." Dee happily said,

"Since both our names begin with the letter D, I decided to keep the family tradition going. Devina and Devika, both of their names mean goddess." Dasia was beaming with joy.

"Baby I love their names and we're going to raise them to be goddess that they are." Dee kissed Dasia again. She told Dee to call everyone in her and his family about having the twins. Dee was extremely happy to be a father.

Dee watched his set of twin baby girls from behind the glass window. That was as close that he could get to them. The nurses told him that it was too early for the twins to be around anyone else germs. It was hard for him to watch Devina and Devika lying in the incubators with tubes running through their tiny little bodies. They couldn't leave the hospital until they were five pounds. Dee was so engulfed with his newborn twin girls that he didn't hear anyone walking up behind him.

"Congratulations my man is a father now." Tavion embraced his best friend Dee with a hug. As soon as Tavion heard the news he rushed to the hospital. He wasn't expected to hear that Dasia had the babies so early.

"Those my daughters right there," Dee cried tears of joy. "I just wished that my brother was here for this moment."

"He's here with us in spirit brother. Aye so you and Keith did that move this morning without my knowledge." Tavion went straight to the point.

Dee turned around to face him. "Yeah we did, funny thing is that I didn't think that we needed your say so before we made a move."

"Look it's not about getting my permission. It's about moving smartly. Sloppy moves means that you have to clean up a lot of bullshit in the long run. In the future discuss any moves that you make. We could've handle that in different way, with less casualties." Tavion replied.

"No offense Tavion but I'm tired of sitting back and waiting. Tyrese and his bitch Emani still out here breathing while Jay is motherfucking dead. I'm not going to stop moving until I get them. Everyone that was involved will pay for the death of my brother." Dee was livid.

Keith interjected before things got out of hand, "We can discuss this later. Right now it's about the twins and Dasia."

They put their differences aside for now. Tavion had said enough and nothing was needed to be said anymore on that matter.

Chapter 12

Sunshine

I was healing and getting better with the help of the awesome doctors and nurses here in the hospital. The only person who I had by my side was Aunt Marci. She was very helpful spiritually and emotionally. I held so much hate in anger inside of me. Revenge was the only thing on my mind. I wanted Tyrese and Emani to pay for everything that they did to me. That's why I agreed to take the deal that was offered to me. There was no way that I was going to sit in jail for the death of the man who I loved when I didn't pull the trigger. A week ago I called Detective Carr after my Aunt Marci encouraged me to do so. Trust me the last thing that I want to do is become a snitch. All I had to do was give my statement and show up to court. With my deal came relocation afterwards. I was good with that because I was ready to get the fuck out of Chicago. From what I heard out in the streets was that Tyrese and Emani was on the run from another apparent hit that went wrong. Detective Carr arrived at the hospital because I was still hospitalized to take my statement.

"Hello Melinda, thanks for cooperating. You've made a wise decision." Detective Carr said as he pulled out a tape recorder.

"Yeah whatever, let's just get this over with." I replied back slowly. Aunt Marci was sitting next to me holding my hand she whispered in my ear *"Be nice Sunshine."*

I rolled my eyes. I wanted do make this quick, Detective Carr started asking me questions. That was easy to do and answer. He asked me to describe the night of the fatal robbery. That's when I had to take a moment to pause. "It's okay Sunshine, just take your time." Aunt Marci said.

A tear trickled down my cheek as I rekindled that awful night that occurred. Flashes and the sound of the gun replayed over in my mind. Duke and I getting shot multiple times made the tears fall. When I was done I was unable to speak for a moment. Detective Carr turned off the tape recorder. I thought that he was done until he pulled out some pictures.

"Melinda do you know anyone of these men?" He asked me.

He showed me pictures of the individuals from the South side of Chicago. Honestly I didn't know of any of them but heard of them. I've seen them around town flossing and getting major paper.

"No I don't recognize them." I replied.

"Thank you so much for your cooperation. I'll be back in touch with you regarding the case." He handed me my paperwork and his card before leaving.

I pushed my emotions to the side taking a look at Aunt Marci. "I need a lawyer. Just in case they try to play my ass." I said.

"I'll get you one. Enough of all that for now. I don't want you to get your blood pressure up." Aunt Marci took a look at my blood pressure on the machine.

"I'm good, it's just hard thinking about Duke. On a better note look at what I could do." I lifted both of my legs one by one slowly.

Aunt Marci smiled at, "Good job Sunshine." She gave me a big hug.

"Thank you, the doctors and physical therapist said that I should be walking by three weeks." I replied.

"Sunshine you got this. When all of this is over you'll be a new person."

Aunt Marci was the most positive person in my life. She could fall down seven times, get back up and take off as if she never fell.

"I'm blessed to have you here with me. After all these years you've never left my side. Even though you're my aunt, you've always been a mother in my heart." Tears started to fall in my hospital room.

Aunt Marci choked on her tears, "Sunshine you'll always be my daughter no matter what your birth certificate says." She kissed me on the forehead.

As we both cried in the room it was a knock on the door, **_Knock. Knock._** "Please come in." I yelled for the person on the other side of the door. To my surprised I saw a familiar face that I haven't seen since Duke was alive.

"Hello Melinda, how are you?" She entered with an uneasy look upon her face.

Aunt Marci took a look at me, "Who is that?" she whispered.

My eyes darted from my aunt and back onto Duke Mom. "Hello Mrs. Rice, I'm very surprised to see you here." I softly spoke. Aunt Marci cleared her throat indicating to me that she wanted to be introduced. "Mrs. Rice this is my Aunt Marci. Aunt Marci this is Mrs. Rice. Duke's mom."

They both said hello. My mind is racing as I'm thinking what breezed blew her this way. The awkward silence in the room was broken.

"Melinda I know you're wondering why I am here. I'm here to see how you're doing. I know a few people who work here and they've been keeping me updated on your progress. I remember telling you that I'm a retired Registered Nurse. After I was told that you're tremendously better I wanted to give you a visit." Mrs. Rice replied.

"Please have a seat, make yourself comfortable." She took a seat in the empty chair. That explains why I have been receiving all this special treatment. This lady old lady had some pull around this hospital. The last time that I saw her was when Duke and I had dinner at their home. That was actually the weekend before his was killed. Now she was seating her in my face, for whatever reason that was.

"How is Mr. Rice doing?" I asked her.

"He's doing well and send his regards. You're looking much better. Before I start to blab my mouth I first want to address that I'm here to support you. I know how deeply he was in love with you. As a matter of fact right before those demons killed my son, he had plans on popping the question."

At that moment my heart stopped racing. I relaxed, no longer panicking wondering what she was doing here.

"Mrs. Rice your son did propose to me that night." I rubbed my naked ring finger.

"Oh my, I didn't know that. Melinda I'm very sorry to bring it him up, I know that talking about this can bring back sweet memories that may be hard for you. Lord knows it has been extremely hard for me and my husband. He was our only son, he didn't have any children. He's gone forever, not leaving his legacy behind. When I look at you I see and feel him. You were the woman who had his heart."

Wow that's was such a surprise to hear. When Duke was alive he would take me by his parents' house a few times to have dinner. I and his mom got along pretty well, but I never expected her to visit me. Having her seat in the chair across from me made me think about Duke. Damn I truly missed him so much. Aunt Marci tapped me on the shoulder knocking me out of my day dream.

"It's no problem at all Mrs. Rice. You're more than welcome to visit me. As a matter of fact you being here will help me out. It may even spend up my healing process."

Mrs. Rice smiled, "I have nothing else to do. Sunshine I'll love to help you out several hours of the day."

Aunt Marci sat there smiling not saying much. "Sunshine I'll leave you two some privacy. Love you, Muah." She gave me a kiss on the forehead before exiting. She allowed me and Duke's mom to catch up on a few things.

The sight of Mrs. Rice made me feel as though Duke was around. He would always hold a special place in my heart. No man has never loved and cared about me like he did. I feel as though I was being cursed for all the bad moves that I've made in the past. God took him away and left me here on earth to suffer. The bullet to my head almost paralyzed me, somehow I was given another chance to live. Mrs. Rice made herself comfortable inside my hospital room.

"Melinda I'm happy that you pull through." Mrs. Rice expressed how she felt.

"Mrs. Rice please call me Sunshine. I never really liked my real name." I shared with her.

She smiled and continued to open up more. "Sunshine I'm happy that you made it. Numerous of times I was up here praying over you without your knowledge. When I heard that someone tried to suffocate you I snapped and made them transfer you on a safer floor. The first thought that ran through my head was that his killers were trying to complete their job by coming up here to suffocate you. I know that my son was involved in the streets, but he never shared with me and his father that he was in any trouble."

At that moment I felt guilty about setting Duke up to get robbed from day one. Here I was fighting for my life and his mother was praying over an accomplice of her son's murder. She shared with me how Duke and his friends felt like I had something to do with his death and wanted nothing to do with me. I always felt as if his friends didn't care for me. When I first met Duke they all shot their shot at me. I turned them down, after that they never really cared for me. On the night he was killed one of his friends slipped his hand under my dress and grabbed my pussy. I checked his ass about it, but never told Duke. So hearing Mrs. Rice share with me how they blamed his murder on me doesn't surprised me at all. The part that fucked me up was that they were right. Duke's mom, a God fearing woman took my side and told them that they were wrong.

"Sunshine sweetie, are you hear with me?" Mrs. Rice snapped me out of my train of thought.

"I'm sorry Mrs. Rice, sometimes I do that. It's may be the medicine that they're giving me causing me to block out sometimes." I lied to her.

"Oh, I understand. Don't worry I'll have a talk to your nurse about your medication. I'll see if they could give you something for that." Mrs. Rice smiled and continued to talk. "Detective Carr and I have been in touch during the process of my son's murder. He told me that you gave your statement today."

My heart started racing, fuck! I didn't know that Mrs. Rice and Detective Carr were talking on a regular basics. Now I have to worry about her finding out that I had anything to do with Duke's murder. Shit! If God was keeping me alive to punish me he was doing a good job at doing so. Right now I felt like shit. I have this sweet woman pouring her heart out to me. She defended me when Duke's friends were right. That's why they didn't respect me and tried to fuck me on the low. My eyes drifted off to Detective Carr's card that was sitting on top of the paperwork on my side table. I had to call him as soon as possible when Mrs. Rice leaves.

Knock! Knock! There was heavy knock at the door. Mrs. Rice and I looked at the door. "Please enter." I told the person on the other side of the door.

My eyes dropped when he walked into the room. "I'm sorry to disturbed you Melinda, but I called Mrs. Rice to talk to her and couldn't get an answer." He said to me before making eye contact with Mrs. Rice. "When I couldn't reach you I call your husband, that's when he informed me that you were at the hospital to visit Melinda."

"No problem at all but, Detective Carr I didn't get a phone call from you." Mrs. Melinda searched inside her purse. She pulled out her cellphone and let out a light laugh. "Silly of me, my phone isn't turned on." She laughed.

Detective Carr laughed as well. I sat back watching their cheery asses laugh. In my head I was wondering what in the fuck Detective Carr had to talk to Mrs. Rice about that couldn't wait. "It is totally fine, I'll be very quick. I just wanted to go over a few new developments on your son's case. Tell you what to expect next, we're ready to get this ball rolling." Detective Carr replied.

To get their attention, I purposely knocked my call light onto the floor. Detective Carr stepped over to pick it up. We both locked eyes, I whispered softly. "Please don't tell on me." I darted my eyes at my paperwork so that he knew what I was talking about. He caught onto what I was getting at. Detective Carr nodded his head in agreement as he grabbed my hand. My heart beat slowed down a bit. I didn't want Mrs. Rice to ever find out that I had something to do with Duke's murder.

He turned back towards Mrs. Rice, continuing to talk to her. "With the help of this young woman we're closer on our leads." They both looked at me, I smiled as if I was a fucking saint.

"I was just telling Melinda," she corrected herself. "I'm sorry Sunshine how much I was praying for her. She's such a very sweet girl. Her nor my son didn't deserve what happened to them."

Detective Carr looked over at me, "Yes she's a very sweet girl. You two ladies enjoy the rest of your day. I'll be in touch with you or Melinda if I have any further questions.

I was so happy to see him leave out of my hospital room. How am I going to keep my involvement of Duke's murder under the radar? Mrs. Rice took a look over at me, "Is everything Sunshine, you seemed to look a little worried?" she asked.

"Pray for me Mrs. Rice, I really need you to pray for me." I replied.

Chapter 13

Kamara

This was the longest three minutes of my life. I paced back and forth waiting for the results of my pregnancy test. It's been a month since my last period. Keith and I were fucking everyday despite all the craziness that was going on. Sometimes we used protection but not all the time. To make the situation more badly, I wasn't on birth control. *BEEP! BEEP! BEEP!* The alarm on my cellphone went off letting me know that it has been three minutes. I stepped slowing into my washroom and pick up my pregnancy test. *Ring! Ring! Ring!* My cellphone startled me. It was Tichina calling from her hospital room. I knew the hospital number by heart because we communicate nonstop.

"Hello best friend, what's up with you?" Tichina was in a bubbly mode.

"Girl, I'm pregnant." I blurted into the phone.

"What are you serious? Does Keith know yet?" Tichina voice changed from bubbly to worry.

"No he doesn't I just pissed on the stick and found out. Tichina I knew that this was going to happen." I sounded disappointed.

"Kamara don't beat yourself up for getting pregnant. You're a wonderful mom and Keith is a good man." Tichina made me feel a little better.

I walked down my hallway to check on Karlie, she was still napping. Barbie played on her television watching her sleep. Keeping the television on was the best choice to not wake Karlie up. Tichina continued to give me a pep talk trying to cheer me up. Sadly to say, her words weren't working. I laid across my bed on my back watching my ceiling fan go round and around. Being pregnant right now was not a good idea. I had so many reasons why, Keith being caught up in this bullshit was the main reason. I heard my alarm go off, "Front door."

I panicked, "Tichina, I gotta call you back. Keith is home." I said quickly.

"Okay friend, don't forget to call me back to tell me everything." Tichina laughed.

I sat up in my bed. "Kamara my beautiful where are you?" Keith called out.

"I'm in the room handsome." I yelled back.

Keith walked in the bedroom. "What's up beautiful," he kissed me. The weed smell on him made my head hurt. "What's wrong why are you looking sad? What happened?" Keith jumped up ready to protect me.

"Nothing's wrong, I'm just having a crabby moment." I replied

"What can I do to cheer my beautiful woman up?" Keith kissed me on the neck playfully. He knew that the side of my neck was my hot spot.

"Keith you think you slick." I laughed, "You trying to get some of my goodies?"

"You're my sweet potato pie," he continued kissing me. "Wait hold up, I have to go piss."

Keith jumped out of the bed so fast that I didn't have time to stop him. Shit I left the pregnancy test on the bathroom sink. It was nothing that I could do now except wait for him to come back in the room. I could hear the toilet flush, then the water running. I knew at that moment that he seen the results. Keith walked back into the room holding the pregnancy test in the air. He looked surprised, shocked and confused.

I busted out in tears, "I'm pregnant Keith. I was going to tell you, what are we going to do?" Tears rolled down my face.

Keith placed the positive pregnancy test on the dresser. He wrapped his arms around me. "What do you mean, what are we going to do? We're going to have a baby, a beautiful family. Me, you, Karlie and this one." Keith kissed my flat belly.

"Keith you have to promise me that you won't get caught up in the street bullshit. They already tried to kill Tichina. I'd go crazy if something happens to you." I cried.

"Don't you worry yourself about losing me? Think positive only baby." Keith kissed my belly.

He was taking my pregnancy better than I thought he would. I was nervous about everything. Maybe I was thinking too much, over thinking could ruin all the fun. How would Karlie feel? Having another baby wasn't in my plans. I wanted to go back to school and travel.

"Tomorrow let's start looking for a bigger home off in the suburbs." Keith said.

I looked at him as if he was crazy. "Since day one you've been trying to get me and Karlie out in the boondocks." I laughed.

"Yes, only because you deserve the big house and space. Do you remember telling me that you want a garden? Let me buy you a house for you and my babies." He happily said.

"What about Karlie, you know that I promised her Disney World next year. I'll have a baby and won't be able to leave just like that."

"Where is your laptop?" Keith looked around until he found my laptop. "Here, book the trip right now for next week." Keith went into his wallet to grab his credit card. "Here is my card, book a flight for all three of us."

"Are you serious? What about everything that's happening here? Is it cool for you to go away?" I questioned him.

"Kamara please do as I ask you. I'm my own boss and have nothing planned."

"Before I book the trip first I need to make a doctor appointment. Pissing on stick isn't always 100% accurate. I need blood work and test done."

"Baby call and make a doctor appointment. That's very important, the sooner the better."

I called my doctor at PCC Wellness to schedule an appointment. My doctor had an availability for me next week, on Monday. Keith was excited about my unexpected pregnancy that he was prepared to call his mother and father."

"What are you doing?' Stopping him from dialing his parents. "Wait till we confirm it from the doctor. You can never be so sure with the at home pregnancy test handsome."

"Baby trust me, you're popped off." Keith laughed.

"If I didn't know any better I would think that you wanted to pop me off."

"No, you know that you we're trying to trap a playa like myself. Have a baby by me baby, be a millionaire." Keith was enjoying the fact that I was pregnant.

I snapped my fingers, rolled my neck and eyes, "I got my own money baby." Playing as if I was a ghetto bitch from the Westside.

We both laughed so hard and loudly. Falling out onto the bed in each other arms. I love Keith so much, he brings me so much joy. We were caught in a moment until we we're interrupted.

"Momma, you woke me up." Karlie sweet little voice startled us. Keith and I straighten up in bed.

"Baby girl momma is sorry, come and give me a hug." Karlie ran into my arms, she was still sleepy. Keith moved my laptop out of the way and got out of the bed.

Karlie eyes grew with excitement. "Disney world momma!" she screamed.

Keith and I looked at my laptop which was still propped opened. Mickey and Minne mouse dumb asses were smiling on the screen waving. Now I had no other choice but to book our Disney trip soon.

Monday morning was here, I dropped Karlie off at day camp. Keith and I we're heading to the doctor's office.

"You got me in the hood baby," Keith replied. My doctor's office was on Lake and Lotus. This was neighborhood, the area where I was so it didn't bother me to go here. Keith is from over East, therefore everything out West was hood to him.

I looked over at him as he parked his truck. "Please don't start with the Westside vs Southside battle. Besides I really like my doctor, me and her have created a bond." I explained to Keith.

"Well excuse me, I better stay in my place. I don't want to get jumped on out West." Keith laughed.

He opened up the door for me. There were two way that you could enter, the front door or through the side door. We went entered through the side door, more toward the back of the seating area. We stepped inside it was packed with women, men, teenagers and crying babies. It was a large place, finding seats wasn't hard. I stood in line to check in at the front desk while Keith went to take a seat in the last back row. The receptionist was happy to see me, we chatted for a bit until the next person walked up to the desk. She winked at me and placed my chart in the front of others. I smiled as I walked away to my seat. Keith's facial expression showed that he was ready to go.

"She looked out for me, we shouldn't be in here too long." I whispered in Keith's ear.

"That was nice of her." He replied.

The televisions on the wall played a movie comedy that everyone was entertained by. There was a woman he sat in the front row of us. She was talking loudly on the phone. Those type of people pissed me off, she didn't have to be that damn loud. She caught on to the ugly stares of others indicating that she was too loud. Finally the armed security officer step over and asked her to lower her conversation.

"Excuse me ma'am, can you please be kind enough to lower your voice?" he asked her.

She rolled her eyes, "Hold on girl, give me a second to put my earphones in." she replied to the person who she was talking to on the phone.

The security officer smiled and walked off. The girl voice was a little lower, however we could still hear her because of how close we were seated. I leaned my head onto Keith's shoulder. He rubbed my hand softly. One by one the medical assistant called people in the back to be seen by the doctor. The people who sat by the loudly speaking woman moved to another seat.

"I don't care about yall moving." she mumbled under her breath. "Anyway, Tootie you have to get out of there. Tyrese and Emani aren't doing anything but using you."

My head popped off Keith's shoulder as we peeped her conversation. Could it be that she was speaking of Emani and Tyrese that I know. Keith gave me the eye, he was on the same thing I was on. Now we were listening to this loud mouth bitch conversation.

"Tootie if it's so sweet with you and the white man, then why don't you run off with him? I don't see how you're so comfortable living with Tyrese and Emani like that if you don't trust them. He already got you involved in so much bullshit."

Now I knew for a fact that she was talking about Emani and Tyrese. The name Tootie did ring a bell. I just couldn't remember where I heard that name before. Keith was heated and ready to snatch the bitch up. He pulled out his cellphone to text someone. His text alert went off, I could see that he told someone to meet him up there now.

The medical assistant stepped from behind the door, "Bridget Martin." she called out the next person.

The loud talking woman stood up, "Tootie they just called my name. I'll call you back once I get out of here." She grabbed her purse and went to see the doctor.

Who would've ever thought that we would run into a person that could link us up to everyone? Small mother fucking world. Keith received another text message. He read it, "One of the people are meeting us up here. " I nodded my head.

There was no need for me to question Keith about what was going. I already knew what was coming next. Besides right now was not a good time to talk about it inside of here. Another medical assistant stepped from behind the door, "Kamara Wilson." Right on time, Keith and I both went in the back to see my doctor. The medical assistant grabbed a cup for me to urine in. "Hey Kamara how are you doing and how is little Miss Karlie?"

"I'm doing fine and so is Karlie," I smiled as I replied back.

She handed me the cup, "That's great, okay we need some urine, give me the cup when you're finished and after that I'll try to get you out of here as quickly as I can."

"Alright cool." Keith went have a seat in the room. I went to pee in the cup, flushed the toilet and washed my hands. As soon as I stepped out the medical assistant was waiting by the door. I handed her the cup of urine. "Have a seat inside the room. I'll be inside to draw your blood in a minute."

When I walked down the hall I passed by the loud speaking mouth Bridget girl. You could hear her voice outside of the thin door. My room was right next to hers. I entered inside, Keith was there waiting for me.

"Everything cool?" He asked.

"Yeah, I gave her the urine. Next blood work after than the doctor." I nodded my head at the wall next to us. "You hear her right? At least we know that she's still here." I replied.

Keith spoke lowly in my ear, "My people are already sitting in the parking lot waiting to follow her. Bridget is Tootie's best friend. Tootie is a woman that Tavion used to fuck with back in the day. I'm glad that she didn't see me when we came in from the back because she would've noticed me."

"Oh, that's where I heard that name Tootie from before. I think her and Tichina had a run in at the beauty shop before. She approached Tichina about fucking with Tavion. Wait, so how does Tootie connect with Tyrese and Emani?" I questioned Keith.

"That's what we need to find out." Keith said.

Knock! Knock! There was a knock on my door. The medical assistant stepped inside carrying her specimen collection tray. She was prepared to draw my blood. Keith took his seat back in the chair while the medical assistant did her job. She drew five tubes and placed a cotton ball and band aid over it, "The doctor will be in shortly Kamara." she smiled before exiting the room.

Moments later we heard Bridget outside of the door. It sounded like she was talking to someone and crying. "I'm about to see what's going." Keith didn't stop me from peeping out of the door. Bridget was crying as the doctor assured her that everything was going to fine. Before they could see me I closed the door quietly and sat back down. "She's crying about something, but she's about to leave." I said.

Keith made a phone call, "Aye she's leaving now. She has on all black, slim thick with a black long weave. We still haven't seen the doctor yet, make sure you follow her. Don't lose her, did you holla at Tavion?" he asked the caller.

"Yeah he told me to do whatever it takes to get her." Tory replied.

"You know to hit the line when you're done." Keith told him.

"Here is Miss Bridget now walking to her car. She's getting in a red Acura. I'll hit you and Tavion when I'm done." Tory ended the call.

Keith went back in supportive mode for me. My doctor tapped on the door and walked inside with my chart in her hand. "Hello Kamara, how are you? What brings you in today?' Dr. McMillian smiled. "Hello and who might this handsome man be?" she asked as she took a seat.

I giggled, "Dr. McMillan this my boyfriend Keith. Keith this is my favorite doctor in the world, Dr. McMillan."

"Hello Dr. McMillan I heard so much about you." Keith shook Dr. McMillian's hand. He flashed a smile exposing his pearly whites.

Dr. McMillan was in her late forties, African American and so down to earth. She has been my gynecologist since I've been seventeen years old. She was the only person that knew how many sexual partners that I've had. Not that I've had many. She also knew about the two nasty sexual transmitted diseases that Karlie's father had given me. She was more like a favorite Aunt to me, it will be hard for me to depart from her.

"I see that you requested a blood test to find out if you're pregnant. Well I have some great news for the both of you. Congratulations you're pregnant." Dr. McMillan happily said.

Keith and I were more than happy. What I had to do next sadden me. "Dr. McMillian is possible if you can refer me to a gynecologist? I may be moving quite a distance soon, south suburbs to be exact. Traveling back and forth pregnant to the doctor will be hard."

"I see, I'll hate to see you go. We have so many years, you're like my little niece." Dr. McMillan and I both hugged. "Give me a second, let me print out some doctors for." She left out of the room

Keith hated to see me hurt, "Kamara stay with her. I can feel how much that you two care about each other. A friendship that you two have between a doctor and patient is hard to build. The only thing that I would like to change is the hospital. We're not having our child at West Suburban Hospital." Keith laughed.

"I'm sure that she could change my hospital, thank you for understanding. "He gave me a hug.

Keith went to go get Dr. McMillan, they both walked back inside. Dr. McMillan, Keith and I discussed my next process. I was aware of what was to come next, however this is Keith's first child and time going through this. Dr. McMillan did a great job explaining to him what to expect. She wrote me out a prescription for prenatal pills. Set up my primary hospital to be Northwestern Memorial. My next appointment we will determine how many weeks that I am by doing an ultrasound. We left the doctor office on a good note.

"You hungry bae, my stomach growling." Keith grabbed his belly.

"Yes I want a jerk chicken salad from off Chicago Ave and Central."

"Order two, extra meat on mine." Keith said. We sat in the parking lot of the clinic for a second. Lately he has been doing that. It bothered me, hell I need to know what's going on.

"Bae why are you sitting here? You know lately you've been doing this. What's up, you know that you can tell me."

"Nothing we good, just giving the restaurant time to make our food."

Keith was lying. I don't know what was going on, but I was going to find the fuck out.

Chapter 14

Bridget

I drove home leaving the doctor's office with some fucked up news. How in the fuck did I end up pregnant again? I've been on the fucking depo shot for a year now. Fuck birth control, the morning after pills and all that bullshit. Shit, I can't afford another child. No fucking way that was going to happen. Working at Aldi's wasn't enough money to feed my three boys and pay rent. All three of my son's father were locked up. Maybe I could call my oldest son mom to help me out. She hasn't come through for me in a long time. I usually like to rotate my son's family when it comes to help. Then the nigga that pop me off isn't returning any of my phone calls. It's been six weeks since I've seen that lying mother fucker, talking about he got this and that. By the time that I found out that he was the worker and that he lived with his baby momma and three kids. I had already fucked him like a porn star, nasty and raw. He wasn't getting off the hook his easy. One thing about me is that I don't like to be played. *Screech!!!!!* My Acura wept around the corner fast catching the attention. The eight men looked up from their illegal dice game that they were playing. When they saw that it was me they went back to shooting dice.

"Shoot hundred bitch!" Omar blew on his dice before rolling them.

"Dammam!" the crowd of boys yelled.

Omar bitch ass was winning I see. "You got me fucked up! Why haven't you been answering my mother fucking calls Omar?!" I stood there with my hands on my hips.

Omar continued to shoot dice ignoring me, they all acted as if I wasn't standing there. It was so much money on the ground. My eyes counted about three thousand. "Game over bitch! Give me my money." Omar laughed as he picked up the cash from the ground. The other boys walked off shaking it up with one another.

"I'm pregnant Omar!" I blurted out.

Omar stood in front of me wearing a mean mug. "How much do you need for you and that baby to get the fuck out of my life?"

"You don't mean that," tears streamed down my face. "That's how you feel after all the times that we got up with each other?!" I punched him in the face. My small fist didn't faze him.

"Bitch you lucky that I don't hit women!" Omar threw some money at me and walked away. I stood there crying looking pathetic. A girl that watched everything from her window yelled out, "Girl you better pick that money up before I do!" Embarrassedly, I picked up the three hundred dollar bills and ran off to my car. Omar sped off in his car down the street. This was the last that I will ever deal with these street niggas. Before I pulled off I cleaned my face. I was too beautiful to be going through this bullshit. My brown mocha skin was beautiful. Shape was banging despite that I had three boys. At the age of 28 I still had a chance at becoming some man's wife out here. I applied Carmex to my cracked lips, fixed my fly hair and sped off.

Finding a park on Madison Street was such a pain in the ass. All I want is some buffalo chicken egg rolls from L & B. Finally someone was pulling out of a parking space. My car barely fit into the parking space but I managed to fit in. My stomach was in knots. I didn't know if it was the baby or if I was hungry. As I walked toward the restaurant a few men that drove past blew their horn at me. L & B's was packed as usual, calling in was a waste of time. Before I could grab the door handle someone did it for me.

"Let me get that for you beautiful," he said.

I turned around prepared see a thug opening the door for me. To my surprise I was shocked. Who was this handsome creature standing before my eyes? He brown, 5'9', a low haircut and dressed in a short sleeve white button down collar shirt and blue jeans. His smell was mesmerizing like a breath of fresh air. *"Snap out of your trance Bridget,"* I told myself in my head. "Thank you so much." I politely said as I stepped inside. I stood behind the long line of people who were in front of me. As he stood behind me I played with my weave. Making sure that it was hanging straight down my back. Right now I was happy that I decided to put on my yellow maxi dress. Instead of the boring tank top and shorts to wear to my doctor's appointment. One by one the people in front of me placed their orders. Every small step that I took I made sure to bounce a little bit just so that he could see my ass. My turn was next to place my order.

"Hey, may I have six buffalo chicken eggrolls with a sprite please." I pulled out one of the hundred dollar bills to pay for my food.

"I got this beautiful," the handsome man said. "Please can you give me the same thing that she has?" He paid for our food.

I smiled, "Thank you that was very nice of you. I've never had a stranger pay for my food before." I blushed.

"No problem beautiful," he smiled. Others watched us start our ghetto romance. "How long for our order to be done?" He asked the cook. The cook told him twenty minutes. I walked outside as he followed behind me.

We walked over to my car, I leaned against it. "Now that everyone isn't looking in our faces we could become better acquainted. Thank you again, my name is Bridget. Your name is?"

"Paul," Tory lied giving her a fake name. He had a mission to accomplish. That mission was getting close to Bridget so that she could connect them to Tootie.

"Are you from around here? I don't think that I've never seen you around before." Bridget inquired.

"Actually I was born here but I moved to Atlanta. Right now I'm just up here for personal reasons. You know legal things that I have to take care." Tory was telling her a perfect story and she was enjoying it.

Bridget smiled she already was making plans for Tory aka Paul in her head. She didn't waste any time inviting him back to her place. To her surprise Tory accepted her invite. He grabbed the bag of food and followed her back to her place. She lived in Oak Park, right off Washington Blvd. and South Lombard Ave. I called Tavion to let him know my whereabouts.

"Yo Tavion, I'm about to go up to Bridget's place now. Her address is 202 Washington Blvd. apartment 104."

"Damn player you move fast." Tavion laughed.

"You know how I do, I'm the man." Tory cockily replied.

"I see, Tory don't lay hands on her. Bridget has always been cool when I was fucking with Tootie. Play the role and get all the information out of her that you can." Tavion ordered.

"Gotta boss man." Tory ended the call.

Bridget was standing in front of her building waving for Tory. He grabbed the bag of food and strolled over to her. Bridget lived in a clean overpriced court way building. Tory was impressed with her decorating skills. When he walked inside the smell of Japanese Cheery Blossom was in the air. "Would you like me to take my shoes off?" he asked.

"Yes, please do. Don't worry I just mopped my hardwood floors." She giggled.

Tory took a seat on the grey sectional. Bridget living room was in decorated in grey, yellow and white. She went in the back to where the kitchen was. "The bathroom is back here if you'll like to wash your hands." she yelled from the back.

Her apartment was big and long. Tory followed the sound of her voice as he walked down the long hallway. He spotted the bathroom on his right. After he washed his hands he joined her at the dining room table. Bridget had their buffalo chicken eggrolls on a fancy plate and their drinks prepared. She smiled, "Paul tell me more about yourself?" Bridget took a bite of her egg roll.

"What would you like to know? Ask me anything?" I replied.

Bridget didn't waste any time questioning him. "Are you married? Do you have a woman? How old are you? Do you have any children or baby momma drama?"

"I'm not married, happily single although I do date. I'm 27 and no baby momma drama because I don't have any children."

"Interesting tell me more about the dating part. How is the dating life in Atlanta? Strip clubs and big booty hoes?" she giggled.

"There goes that giggle again," I smiled. Bridget blushed, she was very beautiful. Fucked up that she's involved in this bullshit. "Dating in Atlanta is strange. Every woman is trying to be more than she is. I don't do strip clubs, don't care to throw my money to them hoes. Enough about me tell me about you. I want to know everything about you."

"I'm 28 and have with three boys. Their ages are 12, 10 and 9. All three of their fathers are locked up. Two in federal custody, the other in state. I'm pretty much raising them on my own, sometimes I receive help from their families. I'm a store manager at Aldi's in Northlake. As far dating anyone," Bridget took a moment and became silent. Thoughts of Omar ran through her head. She thought about how he chewed her up and spit her back out when he was done. "I just ended a complicated situation. Let's just say that I had a situationship."

"I get what you're saying. I've been in a few of those in my past." Tory saw the hurt in her eyes. He lighten up the conversation. "What do you like to do for fun? Do you have any siblings, friends or you hang out with a group of girls?" he was trying to get her to mention Tootie.

"I'm a very spontaneous person. I go with the flow and willing to try anything. Well except drugs. I'm not in to that. No sisters or bothers, I'm the only child. Females and I never really got along much. I could count on one hand how many friends that I have. Not many, the closet that I've gotten to a best friend she moved away. Her name was Tootie, she was more like a big sister than anything."

"Sounds like you miss her a lot. Maybe you should go and visit her. Where did she move to?"

"It's complicated, I wish that I knew where she moved to. She got herself in some trouble and ran off. Leaving everything behind and never coming back. Little by little she's becoming nonexistence in my life."

"Don't give up on her, hopefully she'll come around. The next time that you talk to her open up. Tell her how you feel and that you miss her. Then see where it goes from there. By the way, these egg rolls are good." I held up a piece of my egg roll.

"I knew that you'll like them. Look Paul I don't want you to think that I do this often. I just don't invite strangers in my home. It's something about you. I don't know what it is but I'll like to see you again before you go back to Atlanta."

Bridget found herself falling for another man again. This time around she was going to take it slowly. Paul was certainly her type. The question is was she his type.

"Let me take you out to dinner next week to your favorite restaurant." Tory said.

"Sure I'll love that" Bridget

Tory looked at the time on his watch. Bridget caught on, stood up to walk him to her front door. They made a date for next week. Tory aka Paul gave her a hug before leaving. Bridget closed her front door and locked it. She ran to her window to watch Tory get in his car. Next she had to handle her business. She called Plan Parenthood to schedule the soonest appointment for an abortion.

Chapter 15

Tavion

Knowing that I was one step closer to my target was good news. I've known Bridget just as long as I've known Tootie. The difference between the both of them was that Bridget wasn't as grimey as Tootie. Bridget always looked up to Tootie, she was like her shadow. Back in the day everyone was going crazy over her. That was until she linked up with her first guy and got pregnant. Pretty much after that he got grabbed by the feds. History kept repeating itself in her life. Now she was just another beauty in the hood with three fatherless children trying to make it on her own. What Tavion knew about Bridget was that she wasn't a dummy. That's why he warned Tory to take it slow. More importantly he didn't want Bridget hurt and felt that she would lead them to Tootie. Tavion was still out handling business and taking care of Tichina. The phone call from his ex-girlfriend Kenya caught him off guard.

"You have a prepaid call from Kenya Taylor, an inmate from a federal prison. To accept this call please press 5."
Tavion pressed 5 as he sat on Lakeshore Drive in traffic.

"Hello Tavion, what's going on? I've been trying to contact you for two weeks now." Kenya replied. She sounded worried on the other end of the phone.

"I know Kenya. I'm sorry that I've been avoiding you. Did your sister fill you in on everything that's been going on?" he questioned her.

"Yes she has. That shit hurt me to hear about Twin. I cried when I heard about that. Tavion I know that we're not together anymore, but I still hold a soft spot for you in my heart. I'll go crazy if anything happens to you." Kenya wept on the phone.

"Kenya I don't want you to worry about me while you're in there. Shit is crazy out here, I'm a big boy you know that I could handle myself. Twin got caught slipping with a hoe that he thought that he could trust."

"From what I heard that hoe was your woman friend. Tichina is her name correct? How is she doing?"

"Yeah that's her name and she's doing better."

"Tavion does she know about me? Does she know that I'll be home soon?"

"Yes she knows about you. Kenya I will never keep you a secret from any woman ever. You was my first love. My ride or die. I didn't tell her when you were coming home, but I haven't forgot. I have one of my places set up for you. I'm actually looking forward to seeing you."

"Seven more days and I'll be free. Tavion I can't wait, I miss everyone. Out of everyone I miss you the most." Kenya soft voice soothed Tavion.

"I miss you too beautiful."

"Tavion I have to go now, they're calling for us. You be safe out there, I love you."

"I love you too Kenya, one." He ended the call.

Deep down inside Tavion still had a little feelings for Kenya. He wasn't a terrible man, after all she did a bid for him. Never folded and snitched. He felt as though he owed her so much. When Kenya went away for four years and left a hole in his heart. They fell out over him not being there for her during her bid. After two years Tavion poured himself deeper in the streets. The money was flowing in much better. He never neglected Kenya, he kept money on her books. Making sure that she was never without. Kenya needed more than just his money. She needed him to be on point when she called him. It was hard going from hearing his voice every day to hearing it once a week. Eventually the calls went from once a week and was very dry. Kenya's sister kept her in tune with everything that was going on. Tavion made sure that her family was taken care of as well. He thought about how things would be once Kenya came home.

Ring! Ring! Ring! His ringing phone interrupted Tavion's thoughts. It was Tichina calling him from the hospital. His thoughts drifted from Kenya to Tichina. He answered the call, "What's up beautiful? How are you doing today?"

"Hey handsome, I'm doing much better. Therapy went great, much better. When are you coming up here? I miss you so much." Tichina was more cheery than ever.

"I'll be up there soon beautiful. Just had to handle a few things before I had to you. Do you need me to stop off and get anything?"

"No I just need you here with me."

"Say no more, I'm on my way."

Tavion got off at the nearest exit. He decided taking the streets to her instead. As he drove through traffic he thought about a lot. All of this bullshit was getting to him.

He couldn't think right and haven't been getting much rest. Tavion was just as angrier than Dee. He dealt with his anger differently. Tyrese was going to pay for kidnapping his grandmother, killing Jay and for shooting Tichina. Emani and Tootie was going to die as well. Thoughts of torturing them ran in his head. Tottie was foul, that old bitter bitch lost her mind going against me. Silly bitch couldn't move on from me. No amount of money could keep her out of my life. Kenya hated her, she always felt like Tootie had something to do with her case. We were young and getting money, Tootie had to get cut off because of her jealousy against Kenya. She couldn't roll with the punches, getting paid and keeping quiet. Our fucking fling, that's what I called it ended when I fell in love with Kenya. Shit was popping off again now that I'm in love with Tichina. I can't continue to let her live. Tootie knew too much damaging information that could destroy me. She wasn't going to stop until she does.

***

Mount Sinai was busy as usual with shout victims. Security was tripping and on extra alert checking everyone at the entrance. I stood behind a young lady waiting my turn to enter. The tall, stocky armed guard was familiar with me. He knew our routine, slide him a bill and get in with my piece. "What up man?" I spoke as I held my arms in the air to get checked.

"Man another crazy night." He patted me down quickly.

"I see it, take it easy." I shake his hand, slipping him the fifty dollar bill.

He took the money secretly placing it in his back pocket. I walked passed everyone taking the elevator to Tichina's room. When I approached her room her doctor and parents were present.

"Baby!" Tichina smiled as she shocked me with her next move. She got up and walked to me.

"You're walking? Baby look at you." I hugged her excitedly as I embraced her in my arms.

"I have good news, the doctor is discharging me. Looks like I'm going home." Tichina happily said.

Her parents stood by watching us both. From the look on her mom face she didn't seem too pleased. "How are you doing Mrs. and Mr. Jefferson?"

"Fine Tavion. It's really good to see you again." Mr. Jefferson said. His wife spoke quietly to me, never really giving me much eye contact. She still had her reasons for blaming me about the things that happened to Tichina.

I don't blame me for what happened to my girl. Her hating ass best friend and her man plotted against her to get to me. You tell me who harmed or never gave a fuck about Tichina. I promise you one thing how her parents felt about me wasn't stopping shit from me and Tichina from being together. Finally she was better and ready to get discharged from the hospital. I grabbed all of her belongings preparing to go. The doctors gave Tichina strict instructions on what to do while at home. Personally I was just as excited as her that she was being discharged. I could keep a better eye on her at home.

Mr. Jefferson looked at me sternly in the eye, "Tavion this is very hard for me to allow my daughter back in your presence. I trust that you won't let this happen again. You understand me."

Taking a look into both of Tichina's parents eyes I replied, "I will do everything in my power to keep your daughter safe. I will protect her at all times."

"God dammit you better or else I will kill you myself!" Mrs. Jefferson promised me.

"Maaaaa!" Tichina rushed over by her mother side. She whispered something in her ear. Her mother calmed down. Mrs. Jefferson regained her composure.

"Mrs. And Mr. Jefferson you are more than welcomed to visit your daughter anytime. My home is your home."

"Tavion we shall visit our daughter every Sunday, that's my word." Mr. And Mrs. Jefferson hugged Tichina sadly as if she was going to jail. They were making such a happy moment into a bad one.

I remained quiet until we got into the car. Tichina knew that I was pissed off about her damn parents. "Go ahead, don't hold back tell me what's on your mind," she said.

It's funny to me how she knows me so well. "Your parents will hate me for the rest of their lives because of something that I didn't provoke. That's fucked up and I won't have them do that."

"Tavion they'll get over it, give them some time." Tichina grabbed my hand.

"Rather they get over it or not I really don't give a damn." I continued to drive on our route home. Her biblical parents weren't going to crucify me. I had too much important shit on my mind.

***

Tichina went against doctors' orders taking it upon herself to make love to me. I miss her wet tight pussy while she was hospitalized. She rode my dick slowly not wanting to cause any pain to herself. We looked into each other's eyes. I don't know what happened next, all of a sudden I no longer saw Tichina. Kenya appeared riding me, bouncing up and down on my dick. It felt like the old days when Kenya was my woman. She always loved to ride me, get on top. Tichina thrusted harder and harder on top of me causing me to nut.

"Damn Kenya baby you still got it!" I yelled out.

"Nigga did you just call me Kenya?!" **Smack**! Tichina angrily jumped off of me. Her beautiful succulent breast bounced up and down. Shit! I fucked up.

"Baby you tripping out." I grabbed the side of my jaw. Her small slapped had some power to it.

"No I know what the fuck I heard. You said that bitch Kenya name!"

"You know that you've been through a lot. You're on a lot of medication. You hearing things, chill out."

"Tavion I was skinned in the head by the bullet, not shot in the head. So don't tell me to chill the fuck out!" Tichina threw on a pink tank top. She got in my face," Tell me what the fuck is going on? Have you been back talking her while I was in the hospital?"

Before I spoke I thought about the right way to drop this news on her. "She's being released, next week." Better to just tell her the truth.

Tichina began to go in a dramatic role. "When were you going to tell me? Huh when the bitch was out?!" She was crying and sobbing. "Where is my pain mediation at? I need my medicine!" She grabbed the side of her head.

Chapter 16

Tichina

This nigga had me fucked up, where in the hell is my OxyContin? I shuffled through my bag of items that I brought home from the hospital. The pain in my head was throbbing. I found the pain bottle and popped me a pill rinsing it down with water. I wish that I had medication for the pain that I was feeling in my heart. I stood in the bathroom mirror staring at myself as Tavion knocked on the locked door. *Who was I? What have I gotten myself into? Who was he?* Silently I questioned myself. *Get a hold of yourself Tichina.* Tears ran down my face as I unlocked the door. Tavion reached out to hug me. "Don't you dare touch me?" He didn't, he watched me walk back into the bedroom. My headache was going away. "Tell me truth, don't hold anything back." I requested. If I was going to fuck with Tavion I had to know about my competition. Yes I felt that she was my competitor. "Why are you quiet now? Five minutes ago you were screaming out her name?"

"You're overreacting Tichina. Once that she was released I told you that I was going to look out for her." Tavion sat at the edge of the bed.

"Looking out for her as far as what, fucking her?" I was showing my jealous side right now.

"You know damn well that's not what I meant by looking out for her. Kenya and I closed that chapter in our lives. It's fair that I hit her off right with some cash and a place to stay. Tichina if the shoe was on the other foot. I'll do the same for you."

"So that's why you're calling me Kenya while I'm fucking you? Just admit it, you're still feeling her. I knew that this was going to happen. Kenya coming home and picking back up where she left." I cried.

Tavion held me, "I give you my word that I'll never fuck back with Kenya again. It's about you now gorgeous." He kissed me on my forehead.

"Does she know about me Tavion?" This is the question that I always wanted to know.

"Yes she knows about you baby. It's two in the morning. Let's get some rest, you know that you can't let yourself get worked up."

"This shit isn't over with Tavion. First thing in the morning we'll continue this discussion." I laid down separating us with blanket between us. Tavion wasn't allowed to grind his dick up against. That shit will only make me weak.

***

The time on the alarm clock on the nightstand said 11:37 am. Damn that OxyContin had me knocked the fuck out. Tavion wasn't in sight. He probably was in one of the five bedrooms in this 3,100 square foot home. I slipped my foot into my satin slippers and slapped on my satin robe. First thing that I did was take care of my hygiene before I had my morning coffee. As I at stared at the woman in the mirror she looked different. I saw another woman, a jealous woman. I've never been the type of woman to get jealous about any woman. This Kenya woman was bothering me. Tavion and I wasn't done with our conversation. He wasn't get off easily when it came to her. The closer I got downstairs I heard voices; a familiar female voice to be exact. Just as I thought, Kamara worked her way on this side of town.

Their backs where turn away from the stairway, "Good morning everyone." I startled them both. Disturbing their conversation about me. I pretending like I didn't hear them say my name.

"More like good afternoon sleeping beauty." Kamara smiled, she seemed happier.

Moments later Keith walked in carrying trays of food. "Hello Keith, I didn't know that we were having brunch." I looked from Keith to Tavion.

"All of this wasn't planned honey." Tavion kissed me as if we weren't into it.

"Well let me go upstairs and change." I pulled Kamara away from the table as we ushered off to the bedroom.

I was more than happy that she was here so that I could share my problems with her in person. As I dressed I told her everything that happened last night. You know that my best friend took my side. The one thing that I left out was that he called me Kenya during sex. That was something that I will never tell anyone. That shit was beyond embarrassing to repeat.

"Tichina I know for a fact that Tavion loves you. It's not like he's asking you and Kenya to be friends." Kamara explained.

"Easier for you to say that, you don't have to worry about none of Keith old flings." I dressed in something causal. "You look different too." I stared at Kamara very hard. She just sat there smiling, grinning from ear to ear. "That pregnancy got you glowing already?"

Kamara laughed. "Come on let's go downstairs to eat. I'm super hungry."

Kamara jumped up and walked out the door. Step by step I thought about Tavion and our relationship. My mind was all on the wrong bullshit. When we got back downstairs Tavion, Keith and Tory were sitting at the table. They were talking about Tyrese, Emani. Tootie and someone named Bridget. I spoke to Tory before I started to eat. Tory was cool a young boy that I knew from the streets. Small world that he rotated with Tavion. They filled me in on what the next move was. At this point I didn't have a say so on Emani's death. Those caring feelings disappeared while I was laying in the hospital bed. There was no secret that I always hated Tyrese and didn't care for Tootie.

"So you really think that Bridget will guide you to Tootie?" I asked Tavion.

"Yes Bridget is gullible at times. Trust me she would lead us straight to them all. And if that doesn't work we'll give Big Momma a visit." Tavion replied.

I swallowed the sip of coffee. Kamara and I looked at other. Tavion. Keith and Tory picked up on it. "What's up? Why yall looking like that?" They questioned us.

"Big Momma don't have shit to do with this. However if you do have to go that route just don't kill her. Please don't draw her into this." I begged them.

Big Momma was seventy nine years old. She was raised all her children and grandchildren the best way that she knew how. Only a handful of them made her proud. She shouldn't have to suffer because of Emani foolishness.

"If you're going to go after anyone. Go after Tyrese's losing ass family." Kamara blurted out. "They loose square begging asses." She laughed.

Shit was about to get real if they planned went through. Honestly I'd rather Tavion get to them before Twin does. Dustin was out for bloodshed not giving a fuck about who was killed. They took apart of him when Jay was killed. Tavion explained that Dee wasn't aware of this new tip. They didn't want to involve him until they had them all. Dee rampage will fuck everything. Bridget would fuck around and get killed in the process and Tavion didn't want that. We all ate and discussed the plan. I was down for whatever, ready for all of this shit to be over. I trust that everyone will move smart. I couldn't lose my man to the streets forever. Tavion's phone rang, it was close enough for me to see who was calling. Unknown displayed on his phone screen. He answered his phone, excusing himself from the table. My messy insecure ass crept off behind him seconds later. No one knew what I was except for Kamara. Tavion stepped on the patio closing the glass door behind him. A closed door wasn't going to stop me from stepping on the back. I made myself present. Her name rolled off Tavion's tongue in slow motion…..."K…en….ya" The next move what I did was petty. Grabbing Tavion's phone out of his, I took it upon myself to introduce myself.

"Hello Kenya. I'm Tichina, Tavion's woman. How are you?" I asked her without attitude. Besides I didn't want to waste her minutes arguing on the phone.

"Hello Tichina. I'm fine thanks for asking. How are you doing?" Kenya asked me back. She waited on the end of the line for my response.

Quick Tichina, say something back. The thought ran in my head, what to say next. I wasn't expecting her to respond back that way to me. Damn! I was waiting for a smart remark and then I hit her back with a smart rebuttal. "Tavion tells me that you're set to be released next week. I'm sure that you're excited about that."

"Actually in three days to be exact. I'm super excited that all of this is finally coming to end."

"I was just Tavion that I can't wait to meet you. He told me so many nice things about you." I lied, Tavion light skinned turned red.

"Funny, I was thinking the same way. Tichina I can't wait to meet you either." Kenya was being funny, nasty nice. I picked up on it. "Okay, meet you soon. I'm giving the phone back to Tee now, Nice talking to you." I passed the phone back to Tavion.

You could see it all over his face that he was upset. He finished up his conversation with Kenya while I sat by his side. When he ended the call the fireworks began. "What is your problem? You had no right to fucking do that!" the vein on the side of his forehead popped out.

"Oh so you're cursing at me now, over that bitch? See I knew that she was going to a problem."

"No you're the problem and overthinking shit. Being extra, messy and insecure doesn't look good on you. Here I was thinking that you were different Tichina. I thought that you were mature, what you did was some teenage girl bullshit."

"Fuck you Tavion! I'm leaving so that you won't have to deal with my immature ass!" I tried to walk off, he grabbed my arm.

Through clenched teeth, Tavion whispered in my ear. "You're not going anywhere. Take your ass back inside and we'll deal with this later after everyone leaves." He ordered me.

This was the first time that Tavion has displayed any type of anger toward me. Right now I obeyed him and went inside. Rushing past everyone I went upstairs; not wanting to face them. I buried my head in my pillow crying. Kamara walked in to check on me as I was sobbing.

"Tichina what's wrong? Tavion came back in there looking mad and shit." She rubbed my back comforting me.

"I don't want to talk about it right now." I cried.

"We don't have to talk about it. You know that I'm always here for you."

Kamara sat there as I cried. I made a damn fool of myself over that nothing ass bitch Kenya.

Chapter 17

Keith

Tavion shared with me in private the problem that he was having with Tichina. I'm not the type of man that gets into other people's relationship business. Hopefully they get that shit together. I love Kenya like a sister. She was there since the beginning and did that bid for Tavion. That was some real love right there. Nowadays bitches will flip and snitch on you. Don't get me wrong I rock with Tichina. But Kenya is family and will always be no matter what.

The ride on the way home was a quiet one between Kamara and me. This is the shit that I don't like. When my woman's friend relationship affect ours. Kamara looked out of the window as I drove. I knew when her favorite song, 'Cranes in the Sky' came on and she didn't sing; something was wrong. When I was stopped at a right light I took a look at her, "What's going on baby?" Kamara looked over at me.

She spoke softly, "You know when my best friend is hurting, so am I."

"I always felt that it was best to stay out of people's relationship." Kamara rolled her eyes before she turned her head. She stared out the window, "Fuck that shit, Tichina is my business. You and I both know what is going on. If Tavion hurt my bestie it's going to a problem. And, if that bitch Kenya on bullshit she can get it too."

"You have no idea what you're talking about Kamara. Trust me it's not that deep. Where are we picking Karlie up from?"

Kamara snapped and rolled her neck, "Don't you change the subject up on me. I hate when you fucking do that Keith," she snapped.

I didn't know that I did that until now. Kamara talked shit all the way home. Like the man that I am I remained quiet. When we got to her home she jumped out of my truck quickly walking toward the front door. That's when I noticed a person dressed in all black jumped from out of the bushes. The assailant grabbed Kamara quickly placing a gun to her head,

"Help me Keith please," Kamara cried.

"Shut the fuck up bitch before I kill you." The female assailant warned her. She was taller and thicker than Kamara. I didn't recognize her at all. She dragged Kamara closer to the front door. "Bitch open up the door now!" she kept the gun pointed to her head. I looked around to see if she had anyone with her. It appeared to be that she was working alone. "Keith, if you try to pull some shit, one shot to the head and she's gone." Kamara unlocked the door and we stepped in. "Get down on the fucking floor, keep your hands behind your head."

We did what she told us to do. I looked over at Kamara, she was shaking. My piece was in my placed in my back. I gave Kamara a nod. "Who are you? Why are you doing this? Who sent you?" Kamara asked questions to distract her. The female cocked her gun aiming it at Kamara's head. "Oh you want to be the first to die?" stared coldly into Kamara's eyes. She took one step back stepping on one of

Karlie's dolls. That was chance to grab my piece. "Shit!" her eyes were filled with fear now that a gun was pointed at her head,

"Who sent you?" I asked her.

She swallowed before taking a moment to speak. "Tyrese.

That bitch ass nigga sent a woman to do his job. "Where in the fuck is he?!"

"I don't know where he is. I got a phone call and paid to do what I was told." The look in her eyes told me that she was telling the truth. Those were her last words before I pulled the trigger. Her lifeless body dropped onto the floor. Kamara sat on the floor shaking and crying. I hated to do that in front of her. Being that she is pregnant, she threw up the last meal that was on her stomach. I checked her pockets, the only thing that she had on her was a cell phone. I took the cell phone and went through it. After going through her call log, it was a series of numbers with out of town area codes. I took out my phone to hit up Tavion. "We have a problem, meet me in Westchester now." While Tavion was on the way. I took the body out to the garage.

"Pack some things baby for you and Karlie. We have to move to my place." Kamara moved slowly up off the floor. I helped her up assuring that everything was going to fine. We packed as much as we could in different suitcases. Whatever she needed I will buy. "I'm sorry that you had to witness that. You can leave now, pick Karlie up and go to my place."

"I don't want to leave you. What if something bad happens to you? No, I'm not leaving without you." Kamara wiped the tears and snot from her nose.

"It's best that you don't be here. Trust me I'll be straight." I picked up the suitcases carrying them out to her car. Kamara had to leave, it wasn't a choice. She followed behind me, pouting like a spoiled brat. "You're pregnant and was close to losing your life. Go ahead, I'll call you after I'm done."

"Keith I love," Kamara hugged me tightly as if this was the last time that she would see me alive.

"I love you too baby girl. Call me when you grab Karlie and get to my slot." I kissed her and help her get in the car. Kamara drove down the street slowly.

God was on my side today. Shit certainly could've went left. That's why I didn't feel safe with any of living here. Thirty minutes later, I heard someone pull up in the drive way. I peeped out the blinds. It was Dee. Tavion had to call and tell him what happened. I opened up the door.

"What's good? I heard we had a situation." Dee was ready for whatever.

"I took care of it. Ty hoe ass sent a weak bitch after us. I asked her if she knew where he was. No luck with that."

"Our people should be here with the truck soon." Dee and I chopped it up until our clean up people arrived.

That's what we called them if we needed to clean up a mess. Al the older white guy arrived ten minutes later. He worked alone and was on our payroll. He has been in the business for many years. Any time that you needed someone to go away he was the man to call. His price tag was cheap. He prices started off at fifty thousand. Al backed his van up into the garage and I closed the door. "Where's the body?" he asked.

I kicked the black construction bag. Al picked up the dead body and threw it in a blue bin. What happens after that we don't know? For many years no bodies have been traced back to anywhere. "Nice working with you. Tell Tee I said what's up," Al replied as he got back in the van.

"Likewise, will do." I said as I opened up the garage door. Al pulled off until we needed him again.

Dee turned to look at me. "Almost caught you slipping man. This shit is getting out of hand. Keith I already loss my brother. I can't lose another one."

"We may be closer to him then we expect." I informed Dee.

Dee was pumped up, "How close we talking because I'm more than ready."

"Bridget been back in tune with Tootie and may know her whereabouts. We sent Lil Tory on her to find out."

"Well what did he find out? What are we waiting for?" Dee was more than ready to get shit started.

"Shit nothing much, I do think that we do need to apply more pressure."

"Do you think that she knows more than she's telling us?" Dee questioned me. He may have a point there.

"It's time that we visit Bridget."

I called Tory and told him to meet me in front of Bridget's place. I and Dee drove to Bridget place. Tory was sitting parked out front. He already spoke to her and she was expecting him. We followed Tory to the front the door. He pressed the button, she buzzed the door so that we could enter. We walked up some steps until we reached her door. Bridget opened up with a surprised look upon her face.

"Keith, Dee; what are you doing here? Paul, I didn't know that you knew them." Bridget took a step back allowing us to come in.

We all took a seat on her couch. "What's up? What's going on?" Bridget was from the streets and knew that seeing us had something to do with her friend.

Dee spoke first, "Bridget we're here to find out about your best friend Tootie. Have you seen or heard from her?"

Bridget looked at all three of them, "I need ten thousand cash if you want me to help you."

"No problem if you deliver, ten thousand is yours." I said. Dee nodded his head in agreement. "Tory you know where to get the money from. Go get that and we'll be sitting here waiting on you."

"Alright." Tory replied.

Bridget looked confused, "Tory, I thought your name was Paul?"

Tory looked at Bridget, "Sorry that you had to find out the truth like this." He turned to leave out the door but she stopped him. Bridget became upset, rolling her eyes and was seconds from going off. "Look don't be that way. I still like your sexy ass. Just be cool." Tory left out to get the money.

Bridget, Keith and Dee all sat around talking about everything that was going down. She trusted them and was comfortable doing what she was doing. "I know that Tootie is my girl, however the shit she did was foul. When she started fucking with that nigga Tyrese she changed. I never liked him. One day he had the nerve to ask me to get down with them. I told his ass no way! I don't roll like that. Tootie on the other hand felt cool with setting up niggas. That's when I fell back and stop fucking with her. Never in a million years would I've thought that yall would be a target."

"Yeah I always wondered why you fucked with her." I questioned Bridget.

"At the time she was a woman that I admired. Tootie changed, she didn't use to be a money hungry bitch. It's like her appetite for money grew to a point to cross whoever. You know in the back of mind I always felt like she was never a real friend to me. I was more like her shadow, until that moment when I fell back. Now its fuck Bridget or I deal with Bridget whenever."

Dee cracked his knuckles and replied, "I never liked the bitch. I wanted Tavion to get rid of the bitch years ago."

"Oh trust me Dee that I know. It wasn't a secret that she hated you and Jay, she use to always say I hate those damn twins. I wish that someone would kill those bastards. And Keith," Bridget stopped to laugh. "She low-key liked you and wanted to fuck you. Always use to say, I should fuck Keith to get back at Tavion. Tottie was a real foul dirty bitch." Bridget shook her head. She pulled out her vibrating cell phone from her back pocket. Taking a look at the screen, her eyes grew with excitement. "Yall I think this is her, it's a private call." Bridget said.

"Answer it," I requested her to do.

Bridget placed the phone call on speaker. She held up her pinky finger to her lips telling us to be quiet. Dee and I nodded our heads. The voice indeed was Tootie's on the phone. Bridget played it off as if she was chilling and relaxing. She allowed Tootie talk about what was on her mind. Something about her fucking rich niggas for money. That spoke about that for a minute. Finally Tootie switched the conversation up on Tyrese. Bingo! Now we were getting somewhere. From the conversation Tootie was planning on crossing Tyrese too. There was a notebook and pen on Bridget's end table. I grabbed it quickly and wrote down the questions I wanted her to ask. Bridget took the notebook from me and went into interview mode.

"Tootie where are you? It's only right that you tell someone just in case things go left. You know that you can't trust no one but you can trust me."

"Bridget I'm so confused right now. I don't know what to do. Right now Tyrese is just sitting back calling all the shots and making all the money. I'm considering just running with the money that I have tonight and never coming back."

"I think that you should do that. Tyrese don't give a fuck about nobody but himself. Pretty soon you'll end up dead just like everyone else that he fuck with. You better get out while you can."

Tootie became quiet on the phone for a moment. Bridget called her name out. You could hear Tootie crying and sniffing. She muffled, I'm in Galena about three hours away. Tonight I'm running off and never looking back."

"Where are you running off to friend? You can't go down south, that's where everyone goes. Maybe you should get a hotel and stay there until you figure out what your next move should be. If you want I will get it in my name, that away Tyrese can't trace you."

"Yes please do that Bridget. Make the reservations now at the Ramada by Wyndham Galena Hotel right off US-20 highway. I'll call you back in about two hours. I gotta go now and fuck this man that I booked with." Tootie was rushing to get off the phone.

"Wait Tootie, before you go I need your number."

"Its 219-444-3559, okay gotta go." The phone call ended.

I wrote down everything that Tootie told her. "You did a good job Bridget. Now make the reservations at the place. By tonight we should be there."

Bridget did what I instructed her to do. Dee was more than ready to hit the road. Between him and Tavion I don't know who wanted Tootie head the most. The doorbell rang, "Who is it?" Bridget asked.

"Tory." She buzzed him in. He walked inside with a Gucci back pack on. Inside the back pack was the ten thousand that Bridget requested.

"Here is your money. If you're smart you'll town." I suggested.

"I'm getting me and three sons out of here. Chicago not about to take them like it did their father's." Bridget replied.

"I trust that you won't tell anyone about this or else your son's won't have a mother either." I warned her.

"Trust me I won't tell a soul." Bridget promised.

Chapter 18

Tyrese

Money was flowing back in with the way that Emani and Tootie was working. These wealthy white men loved black pussy and was blowing up the line to fuck them. When I got news that Maine, Sweety and Tweety was killed; I had to react out. I made a phone call and sent my girl Gaby to handle a job. Gaby job was to kill Kamara, shit since we couldn't get to Tavion or his partner Keith. Emani still knew where Kamara lived and that was perfect. That was two hours ago and I still haven't heard back from her. My mind was on what my next move should be. Everything wasn't going as planned, my next move had to be my best move. Emani and Tootie prepared for their next jobs. At this point I trusted them to move around on their own. They each felt comfortable enough to get up with their tricks with a piece on them.

"Emani bae, I need to holla at you." Emani was in the closet trying to figure out what she was wearing tonight.

She walked out the closet naked, "What's up husband?" wrapping her arms around my shoulders.

"I'm so stressed out baby. Something's not right, I don't know what it is." I shared with Emani.

She was on a natural high, been so damn happy lately. "What are you talking about? Money is finally coming in. What's on your mind?" Emani took a seat next to me.

"I've been thinking about leaving real soon. Packing up and going south like I promised you."

Emani happy smile faded away, "What about our children? Tyrese we can't leave them behind."

"We're not leaving anyone behind. We'll get settled in and then send for them."

"When are you talking about leaving?"

"At the end of this month. We're leaving and starting all over. Look sweetheart." I pointed to the homes that were displayed on the screen. I'm shopping for a home now. We have more than enough money to afford a home and all."

"Ty, those homes are beautiful. Twice the size of this home. What about this home?"

"I'll let you in on a secret. This home is being rented under another person's name that I used. Don't worry about anything, the person is dead." I laughed.

Emani laughed right along with me. That's why I loved her ass, she was my down ass chick. Whatever I did wrong she backed that shit up. Not giving a fuck like me. We both kissed and started back looking at homes on the internet. Emani sat on my lap, my dick harden. She looked at me with a flirtiest look in her eyes. She knew what I wanted, getting down on her knees. Taking my hard dick into her mouth. Emani sleeping with other men was starting to turn her into a little freaky hoe. She sucked my dick ten times better. Even had new techniques that I was pleased with. She was performing one of those tongue techniques now on me.

"Shit girl." Grabbing the back of her hair, I pushed her head down lower. Emani deep throated my dick swallowing it up whole. My nut shot down her throat. Emani swallowed every drop. ***Tap. Tap. Tap.*** Emani got up from her knees, "What's up Tootie," she was standing by the door.

"I didn't mean to interrupt you, I just wanted to tell you that I was leaving now." Tootie was dressed in a sexy white dress. Looking tasty making my dick back hard. Emani peeped my dick rising back up. She gave me a dirty look. I pulled my pants back up quickly.

"Tootie, I'll call to check on you after you're done with your first job."

Tootie rolled her eyes at Emani and turned to look at me, "Cool Ty, and talk to you later." Her thick ass switched out of the room.

Emani hit me in the stomach so that I would stop looking at her. "Baby you know that I'm done fucking her."

"You better be! She's not going with us either. You need to let your girlfriend know your plans." Emani warned me.

"Oh so now she's my girlfriend?" I laughed as I swept Emani off her feet. Looking into her eyes, I told her, "You're my girlfriend."

"Tyrese I swear if you don't make shit happen I'm done fucking with you." Emani was serious.

"I promise baby this is the real move right here."

Emani walked off staring at me. She went back into the closet to find something to wear. I was lying about this not being the real move. Time was running out, I couldn't be caught slipping. Shit wasn't going as planned and I didn't have money to waste. It was time for me to go south, jump down with my cousin and get shit popping. The truth is that I'm losing against Tavion. Running would be the wisest move to make. I couldn't allow Emani to know that I was losing and failing. If I did she would think that I was less of a man. I'll lose control over her and eventually lose her as well. The truth is that I couldn't do it without my Queen. I needed her more than ever now. I just can't let her see me sweat.

The house was quiet, two hours had gone by. My cellphone hasn't rang about any good news. Emani and Tootie were out making money. I was starting to get nervous rethinking that hiring Gaby wasn't a good idea. Usually I would've heard something by now. Nervously I grabbed my duffle bag and went to my stash to pack the cash up. After that I packed Emani and I important items that we would need. Being here too long was too risky. Trip by trip I went downstairs placing the bags into the truck. By the end of the week I and Emani will be out of here. I just had to break the news to Tootie. She couldn't go with us and had to fend for herself.

Chapter 19

Big Momma

"Jesus is on the main line, tell him what you want…Oh Jesus is on the main line tell him what you want. Jesus is on the main line tell him what you want. You just call him up and tell him what you want." Big Momma was busy singing as she cooked her dinner.

Her popular fried chicken had the house smelling good as she deep fried it. The collard greens, and candied yams cooked on top of the stove. While the macaroni and cheese and cornbread baked in the oven. Despite the 90 degree temperature outside, Big Momma still prepared dinner. She had a house full of hungry grandchildren. Big Momma was interrupted by one her youngest grandchildren "Big Momma! Big Momma, it's a white man at the door." he came in running and yelling.

"Okay child, let me go see who's at the door." she washed her hands and dried them off on her apron. Big Momma wobbled to the living room. Her eight grandchildren were quietly standing behind the oldest ninth one that was at the door. They were all eyeing the white man down, not allowing him in the house. "Watch out yall, let me see who there are."

Detective Carr was standing outside on her front porch. "Hello Mrs. Ferguson, I'm Detective Carr. I'm here today to ask you some questions about your granddaughter Emani

Martin. Do you mind if I come in?" he asked flashing his badge.

Big Momma took a look at him up and down. "Come in Detective Carr." Everyone stood back allowing him to come inside. Emani's children Tyrese Jr. and Tyeisha stared harder at the guy. "Yall go in the kitchen and watch the food while I talk to the man." She ordered them. Not talking back, everyone went to the kitchen obeying Big Momma.

Detective Carr and I took a seat on the couch. "How can I help you?" Big Momma asked him.

"I'm looking for Emani, have you heard from her?"

"No I haven't heard from my granddaughter at all. Not since her home exploded. I pray that she's okay." Big Momma lied.

"Do you think that someone is out to kill her as well as Tyrese?" he asked.

"The last time that I heard from Emani she shared with me how Tyrese owed someone some money."

"Did she say who that someone is?" Detective Carr pulled out his tape recorder. "Never mind, I just have to record the information." He explained to her.

Big Momma became a little nervous. She didn't let him see her sweat though. "No she never mentioned a name."

"Can you tell me more about Tyrese? What was he involved in to make people want to kill him?"

"I can't tell you much about Tyrese except for the fact that he's trouble. Maybe his family could help you out when it comes to him."

"His family won't talk, they don't say much at all. The word on the street is that they're not far from here."

While Big Momma and Detective Carr was talking, Lil Ty were eaves dropping on their conversation.

Big Momma sat there quietly watching Detective Carr. She didn't have anything more to say to him. "Grandma your food is burning!" Big Momma got up quickly, "Detective Carr I need to get back to my dinner before I burn my house down."

Detective Carr got up to see his way out. "If you hear from Emani please give me a call." He handed her his card. Big Momma took the card and sent him out the door. She grabbed her chest, "God please forgive me for lying." Her grandchildren were standing in the living room. "Is he gone yet Big Momma?" they asked her.

She took a look out of the window to make sure that he pulled off. "Yes he's gone children. Good job on getting him to go. Now let's get ready to have dinner. Tee Baby, can you help me make the plates."

"Yes Big Momma," Tee Baby replied. She was one of Big Momma's granddaughter. While Big Momma wobbled to the kitchen Tee Baby whispered into Lil Ty's ear. "Call your mom now to tell her about the detective."

After that she went into the kitchen to help Big Momma out. Knowing that making plates for nine children was going to take some time. Lil Ty went into one of the bedrooms to make a phone call. They weren't going to let the people take their parents away from them. Lil Ty made the phone call to his mother, but she didn't answer. That led him to call his father. "Dad a detective just left Big Momma's house questioning her about you."

"Did you hear what they were talking about?" Tyrese questioned him.

"Big Momma said that she didn't know where you were. After that he left, that's all that I heard." Lil Ty told him.

"Okay call me if you find out anything else son. Let Big Momma know that I'm going to send you and your little sister some money in about an hour. Lil Ty I want you and your sister to know that I love you. Pretty soon we will all be back together." Tyrese told his son.

"We love you too dad, take care of mom." Lil Ty told his father and hung up.

Lil Ty was not happy about everything that was going on. He may have been young, however he didn't play about his mother. He hated his father and secretly blamed his father for Tyshawn's death. He felt that he caused all of this craziness to wreck their family. Now their family was split up and their parents were on the run. They loved Big Momma dearly but they wanted their life back to the way things used to be. One big happy illegal family.

After dinner Big Momma cleaned up the kitchen with the help of her granddaughters. When Emani's mother came home she was able to tend to the children. In the privacy of her own room she had time to call Emani. The phone rang three times, "Emani child please answer your phone." Finally Emani answered on the fourth ring.

"Hello Big Momma, is everything fine?" Emani was in the middle of riding a client's dick. She bounced up and down on top of him minimizing her moans.

"No everything isn't okay. A detective came by here today questioning me about you and Tyrese."

Emani stopped riding the man, "What did he ask you? What did you say? Are my children okay?" she started to get dressed. Her 67 year old client watched her and wasn't pleased. He didn't get the chance to get his nut off.

"I didn't say much, you know that I'm not a going to run my mouth. Basically I kept it short and blew him off."

"Great that you blew him off. Big Momma where are my children? Do you mind if I speak to them?"

"Sure baby, hold on." Big Momma banged her right foot on her wooden floor. Everyone knew what that meant when she did that. She wasn't going to yell raising her blood pressure. Nor walk back down the stairs. She jumped back on the phone, "Emani baby you need to come home. Forget Tyrese turn yourself in. Your children need you."

Emani got paid leaving her client unsatisfied. She didn't care, her freedom was on the line. "Big Momma it isn't that easy. I'm more than worried about being alive than doing time. I can never come back home." Tears roll down her cheek as she tapped on the cobblestone heading toward the car.

Lil Ty came bursting through Big Momma's door. "Yes Big Momma you need something? He asked her trying to catch his breath.

Big Momma handed him the phone, "Here child your momma is on the phone."

Lil Ty's eyes lit up in excitement, happy to finally hear from his mom. It has been a week since he has spoken to her. Big Momma sat on the edge of her bed praying silently. She was ready for everything to go back to the way it was. However, Emani just confirmed to her that it may never be the same.

Chapter 20

Detective Carr

Detective Carr squeezed into the small park on Washington Blvd. Earlier today he spoke to Tootie's mother. During the conversation Tootie's mom mentioned her best friend Tootie. She said that Bridget may know Tootie's whereabouts. Standing in front of 202 Washington building he searched for the last name Cooper. He pressed the button, hoping that she was in the house. Moments later a child asked who it was, "Who is it?" Bridget's oldest song asked.

"Detective Carr, I'm looking for Bridget Cooper." The intercom system became quiet.

Bridget opened up her window, she snuck her head out to see who it was. Detective Carr flashed his badge, "I'm Detective Carr from 15th District. I have some question to ask you in regards of Tootie Baker. Do you mind if I come up?"

Bridget rolled her eyes, she wasn't prepared to talk to a fucking detective. "Fuck." She whispered under her breath buzzing him. She straighten up a few things and told her son's to go in their rooms. Detective Carr stepped inside her place peeping out the scene. Bridget Cooper's place was clean and very nice. He was impressed by her living style. "Do you mind if I have a seat?" Bridget stood in front of him with her arms crossed her chest.

"Sure have seat, what you need to know about Tootie?" she already knew what was to come. Bridget acted as if she didn't know anything about Tootie's whereabouts. Honestly she would rather see her dead than to spend time in jail. All the anger that Bridget kept inside came from Tootie fucking one of her baby fathers on the low. When he went to prison he confessed to her in prison that he and Tootie had fucked once. I went to Tootie about it but she denied it and said that he was lying. Why would my son's father lie about fucking my friend? In the past many women have told me to not trust Tootie around my man. Needless to say that I choose my friend over my man which was a dumb choice. For years I've hid the anger and animosity. Not being for certain if the hoe fucked him or not. Until one day when we were both discussing the topic of big dicks. Tootie said that she couldn't take big dicks. Now I usually don't discuss the dicks that I do with friends, especially this hoe ass friend. She slipped up and asked me how could I take my baby daddy big dick. How did this hoe know that his dick was big? I questioned her about it. She replied back saying that it's a rumor about my baby daddy having a horse dick. Lies bitch, you fucked him and now you trying to clean shit up. We stopped talking for a month after that. The only reason why Tootie and I got back cool is because she spends cash on me. So I just use the hoe for the help. It's hard out here with three boys working on an Aldi's salary. Tootie would hit a lick and shop for my boys buying them everything. That's why I was crying to the hoe on the phone about some money while she was on the run. Even though I didn't need the money now because I'm ten stacks richer. I wasn't going to snitch on her to the police.

"Detective I have no idea where the hoe is at. She's no longer my friend, I don't know why her mother would send you here. Now if you'll excuse me, I have to make dinner for my children. Have a nice day Mr."

Detective Carr looked Bridget in the eyes for a moment. He couldn't read her, she was good. Maybe she was lying or telling the truth. He got up to leave respecting her wishes. Bridget wasn't an accomplice or had any reason to be a suspect. "Thank you for all your help, you enjoy dinner." Detective Carr left feeling as if he was just being played. Sooner or later he will catch up with Tyrese, Emani and Tootie; he felt that they were all connected.

Chapter 21

Tavion

Keith and Dee rushed back over here with unexpected details. "So yall telling me that Tyrese is three hours away? Damn all this mother fucking time that bitch ass nigga been close by." I was beyond livid.

"Man you trying to make this move with us or not?" Dee was amped up and ready.

This shit was good news but came at a bad time. Tichina just was released from the hospital and we were still having problems. Right now I didn't want to leave my girl but I had to. I thought about what to do before making a final decision.

Tichina was in the bedroom watching television when I approached her. "Hey bae I need to bust a move right now." I sat down next to her in the bed.

She was still upset with me. "I already heard about everything. I and Kamara just got off the phone." Never making eye contact with me, she continued to watch television.

I picked up the remote control to turn off the television. "Look you need to snap out of your attitude right now. I'm about to take care of some serious business that can go in any direction. I'm going to have three men securing the house. If you need anything tell them. This could take all night so get you rest. Hopefully in the morning you'll wake up with your mind right." I kissed Tichina on the forehead.

She didn't say anything, instead she rolled over throwing the blanket over her head. I left out to join Keith and Dee in the garage. Our driver was already there placing the weapons in our hidden car compartments. Three hours was a ride, we didn't put on our bullet proof vest yet. We jumped in the black Chevy Impala and pulled off. Apart of me felt upset that I was leaving Tichina spoiled ass at home at a time such as this. If it wasn't personal I'll hire someone to whack all three of their asses. This job had to be done the right way. No damn mistakes. I had to make sure that they were dead.

***

The two hours had past and everyone was still up. Dee was actually handling it very cool. He spoke about his newborn baby girl during the hour. One thing that I knew about my partner is that he has changed since the arrival of his daughter. Tonight had to go down without an error. We couldn't risk any mistakes, more importantly lose anyone. We all had people who loved and depended on us.

Chapter 22

Tootie

"Hello I have a reservation, my name is Bridget Cooper." Tootie took the fake Id that she had made with Bridget information on it to check into the hotel. She kept looking over her shoulder as the receptionist punched the keyboard.

"You're all checked in Miss Cooper, pleas enjoy your stay at the Ramada by Wyndham Galena." The young lady gave her the key card.

"Thank you." Tootie nervously rolled her luggage that she managed to sneak out of the house down the hall. She pressed the number two on the elevator. Her room number was 211, she took it up to the second floor. Her hands trembled as she swiped the key card. The door opened, before entering she looked over her shoulder one last time.

Tootie sat on the bed making herself comfortable. She was a nervous wreck but happy to be away from Tyrese and Emani finally. Her body ached and she had to freshen up. Before she did that she sorted through her luggage. Taking out the black plastic bag filled with money. She had her savings and helped herself to twenty thousand dollars of Tyrese money. *I cashed out baby!* Tootie laughed as she counted the money. When she was done she had forty three thousand. That still wasn't enough to change her life. It was enough to be on the run. Tootie didn't have a clue what her next move would be. Relocating to another state was a must. Maybe she can start over in Minnesota. It was slow there and interracial couples were very popular.

A white man doesn't seem too bad. I thought to myself. Time to soak my damn body. This rinky dinky hotel wasn't the Ritz Carlton, it was only temporary. The Jacuzzi was small that my thick ass barely fit into it. Before I soaked I ordered me some food from room service. Shit I was starving fucking out there on an empty stomach. The kitchen told me that my food will be thirty minutes. That was enough time for me to soak my pussy. The hot water felt so damn good. With the white wash cloth and generic soap I washed the four men scents off my body. Following I soaked my sins away. My mind raced as I thought on my next move. Any moment now Tyrese will be calling once he realized that I wasn't back. Finally it was peace and quietness. No more worrying about Emani and Tyrese snake asses.

Thirty minutes passed, there was knock on my door. "Room service," the man replied.

Stepping out of the tub I grabbed the bath towel wrapping it around my body. My thick ass had too much body that the top of my breast and ass were exposed. I opened up the door smiling, "Thank you."

The door man smiled as he admired my bodacious body. That was his tip from me so he knew better than to expect a tip in cash. I closed the door, made myself comfortable and prepared to eat. The juicy fat burger and truffle fries smiled so well. I haven't had a good ass burger since I've been on the run. The grease, ketchup and mustard fell out of the big sloppy burger onto the side of my face. At this moment I didn't care about being pretty. I turned on the television to watch a movie. After I was done from maxing, I drifted off to sleep.

***

Ring! Ring! Ring! I was awakened by the sound of my cellphone. Taking a look at the time I seen that I've been sleep for over an hour. The number was recognizable but I couldn't tell of hand where I knew it from. "Hello." I was tired and irritated.

"Wake up dirty bitch!" Bridget blared in my ear.

"What's up boo, I was tired." I replied as I sat up.

"Are you enjoying your room?" Bridget sounded as if she had an attitude.

"I'm sorry about not calling you when I arrived. Yes I am. I can't help but to thank you for everything, after everything that I've been through you're the only one here for me."

"Well don't be too quick to thank me. I did something that I've been wanted to do for such a long time."

Now I'm confused, what in the fuck is she on? "Bridget what are you talking about? I don't understand. Right now you're not making any sense."

"It's payback bitch for being a fake ass friend. Tavion, Keith and Dee should be showing up any minute now." Bridget laughed.

"What?! How could you do that to me?! You broke dirty hoe!"

"No you're the hoe for fucking my baby daddy! What you thought that I was going to let you slide hoe?!"

"It's cool hoe, I fucked him five times. Best dick that I ever had. Your goofy ass couldn't take care of him so he fucked with a real woman that could."

Bridget laughed. "Typical of you Tootie, the old hoe who could never get anyone to wife her. You're so stupid that you got tricked into becoming a real hoe. Happy dying bitch! I hope they blow your head off!"

Bridget ended the phone call. *Fuck*! I rushed to throw on whatever I got my hands on. Quickly grabbing the cash stuffing it into the bag. I slipped on my shoes, made sure I had my phone and ran for the door. I opened the door, "Fuck!" A gun was pointed to my head.

"Where the fuck you think you're going?!" Tavion grabbed by throat lifting me in the air. With Keith and Dee following behind him they threw me back in the door. Once the door closed I knew that I was about to meet my maker. Crawling away I gasp trying to catch my breath.

Kick! Kick! Tavion kicked me in the stomach twice. "You raggedy pussy bitch! What you thought that we weren't going to catch up with you!" he dragged me.

He and Dee kept their guns aimed at while Keith searched the room for anyone. "Please don't kill me! I'll do whatever it takes to stay alive." I pleaded and begged for my life.

Punch! Dee punched me knocking me into a daze. Everything was now in slow motion. I was falling apart. **Ring! Ring! Ring!** My cellphone was ringing. Tavion answered it holding it to me ear.

"Bitch where the fuck are you?" It was Emani yelling in my ear. I knew that it wouldn't be too long that they'll be looking for me.

I was very weak, couldn't barely move lips. "Help me." I whispered into the phone.

"What? Tootie where are you?" Emani continued to ask me.

Tavion nudged the gun in my temple. "They have me, Tavion is going to kill me." I swallowed my blood and saliva.

Emani hung up the phone. At this point I didn't care about living anymore. I wasn't going to put up a fight or continue to beg for my life.

"Where are they?" Tavion asked me.

Mumbling I gave them the address of Tyrese and Emani's house. Tavion placed a silencer onto his gun. He aimed the gun at my head. I closed my eyes preparing for what was next. **Pop! Pop! Pop!** Three times in my head took me away. My head rocked to the right. Darkness appeared and my life flashed before my eyes. I saw images of me when I was little girl. Some were good, some bad. My mother face popped up, she was sad and crying. Bridget face was displayed, she was laughing wickedly. Some of the men that I slept with in the past faces appeared. They all had a look of treachery upon their faces. My life started to drift away memory after memory. It was dark, so dark that I couldn't see anything but blackness. Where was the white light that I heard about before entering heaven? All I could hear were evil voices, screams and dreadful music. This was my life finale. An evil presence pulled and grabbed at me. I tried to fight it off me but didn't succeed. It was much stronger and powerful. The pain and heat that I felt was unbearable. This is it, I took my last breath. The darkness took me away.

Tootie's body jerked up with her eyes open. Tavion, Keith and Dee have killed many people and have never seen anything like that. Her eyes was dark and cold. Tavion aimed his gun at her chest shooting her in the heart. Blood splatter everyone when her body hit the carpet floor.

"Go your hoe ass to hell!" Tavion angrily said to Tootie one last time.

The three of them exited the hotel room on their way to finish off Tyrese and Emani. Tootie's limped body laid there dead. Ten minutes later the house keeper rolled passed Tootie's room and noticed that her room door was slightly open. She took it upon herself to tap on the door twice. When she didn't get a response the housekeeper step inside. "Oh my God," the housekeeper said as she stepped inside over Tootie's dead body and took the bag of money. Afterwards she pulled out her walkie talkie to report the murder. She hid the bag of money inside her cart just in time before her boss and the other employee's got off the elevator.

Chapter 23

Emani

My heart raced as I sped through traffic. How in the fuck did they find us?! **Ring! Ring! Ring!** *The caller has a voicemail inbox that has not been set up.* Fuck! "Tyrese why aren't you answering your damn phone! *Think Emani, think fast.* Thoughts filled my head. I was fifteen minutes from my home. Right now time and traffic wasn't on my side. I continued to call Tyrese but he didn't answer. Twenty minutes later I arrived to our home.

"Tyrese where are you?!" I kicked off my shoes and ran upstairs. When I looked inside our bedroom I noticed that Tyrese suitcase and some clothing was gone. This bastard bailed out on me. My dumb ass actually believed every promise that he told. My lips quivered and eyes watered up. I chocked on my tears as I gathered my thoughts. My next move had to be my best move. *Please let my stash be still where I hid it.* On the first floor I secretly hid my cash under a wooden panel that I took apart. Quickly I searched for my money and thankfully it was still there. I grabbed it and got the fuck out of the house with only the clothes on my back. Since Tyrese wanted to play mother fucking games with me I'm going to win at this game. I pulled out my phone.

"Hello Big Momma, I'm on my way home to you now." I cried,

"Oh Emani is everything okay? Only you are allowed to come home, don't bring Tyrese to my house." Big Momma warned me.

"Don't worry, I'm coming alone. It will take me three hours to get there. Please don't tell anyone."

"I'm not going to let a soul know. Be safe on the road."

What Big Momma mentioned to me earlier didn't sound like suck a bad idea now. I can't believe that Tyrese flipped on me and skipped town. I called his phone over and over again. He continually sent me the voicemail. Tootie told me not to trust him. Maybe she and Tyrese had plans to run off all along leaving me out of the picture. What puzzling me is how in the fuck did they catch up with Tootie. No one is to be trusted at this point. The only place where Tyrese was headed was down south. I know for a fact how badly he wanted to get down there to start his thing. I wished that I could start all over again. Wish that I would've never betrayed my friends. Here I am running for my life. Putting my family and freedom in jeopardy all for the money. Tyrese never gave a fuck about. He was always for himself and himself only.

Meanwhile

Tavion, Keith and Dee made pulled up to Emani and Tyrese residence. The garage door was open and the front door was unlocked. Before entering they drew their guns. When they entered they separated searching each room. Once they realized that Emani and Tyrese had got out of there.

"Looks like someone had plans to leave town." Keith picked up some paperwork that was on the table. It was a print out of homes that were available for rent in Georgia.

"Nigga's think moving to Georgia gonna save their lives. He still could get touched." Tavion replied.

They took the paperwork and left out of the home. Tavion was furious and wanted Tyrese ass badly. Tyrese running off to Georgia still didn't matter. Tavion had people that he fucked with down south that could grab him. He pulled out his phone to make a phone call. Tyrese wasn't going to live long once he made it there. Tavion gave strict orders to hold them once they grabbed him. He wanted to take pleasure in killing him.

"Our girl Bridget came through with her information." Dee replied.

"Yeah she did, lead us right to them all. If only we would've moved quicker."

Tavion turned down the volume on the radio. Everyone got quiet in the car when the police jumped behind them. They driver kept on driving straight ahead. We weren't worried about anything because we knew that we were legal. The cop continued to follow us for one block before he sped off.

"Damn I thought his bitch ass was going to pull us over."
Dee unloosened up, he was tensed because he had two
more months to finish then he'll be off papers.

The driver laughed, "Bitch ass white boy didn't want no
smoke."

They all laughed except for Tavion. He was thinking about
everything that occurred during the summer. All of this shit
was beginning to take a toll on him. It took away from
being on top of his money. He had dependable people still
running shit, but he was the only person who kept shit
pumping. Then it was Tichina and Kenya situation. All of
this shit was stressing him out. He realized that every move
that he was making was very risky and that he had to be
extra careful. Checking the time on his phone, he saw that
it was going on 1am. Tichina was on his mind as he sat
quietly thinking.

Chicago I'm back bitch! Parking on the block wasn't a smart idea. Keeping a low profile I hit the back alley. Big Momma was waiting on my arrival. She was standing outside in the garage wearing a head scarf, her house robe and slippers. Slowly and quietly I parked my car in the garage. We both crept inside the backdoor not trying to wake anyone. I went upstairs to old bedroom where I grew up in. Tyeisha and Lil Ty were both asleep. *My babies.* The sight of them made all of my troubles fad away. The long three and a half ride had me extremely exhausted. I squeezed between the both of them in the queen size bed. They wiggled close to me without opening up their eyes. Big Momma stood over the bed praying in silence over us. She would always do that early in the morning all over her house. I laid there in silence until I drifted off to sleep.

Someone kept playing with my eyelids and laughing. The two weren't going to stop until I woke up.

"I'm up, I'm up." I stretch wiping the crust out of my eyes.

Tyeisha and Lil Ty sat in front of smiling. "Momma are you hungry? Big Momma made breakfast hours ago but now it's all gone. You've been sleep for a long time. Tyeisha smart mouth butt said.

"Give me a hug, I miss you two so much." I gave them a bear hug squeezing them.

"Momma." They giggled.

"Let me freshen up and then we can go downstairs and have lunch. I will order us a pizza with your favorite from Barney's."

"Okay mom, hurry up please." They both ordered me. I forgot how bossy these two could be.

Twenty minutes later I was clean and dressed in clothing that I wouldn't dare be caught in. I ordered a three large sausage and pepperoni pizza. My other little cousins were over so everyone was going to eat pizza. They were all happy and excited to see their big cousin Emani back home. Of course they had several questions for me like why wasn't I at Tyshawn's funeral. For them to be children they were smart and aware of a lot of things. I answered each of their questions with a lie. They were children and didn't need to know the truth until they were older. When the pizzas arrived I fed everyone. Tyeisha, Lil Ty and I went back to the room to eat in privacy. That was best for us to do. The questions about where their father was and was I going to jail were the first two they asked.

"Where is daddy at mom? Did they kill him? Is he in jail?" Lil Ty was very concerned about his father.

I took a bite of my slice of pizza. "Do you want the truth?" I asked them.

"Yes we want the truth. We're being tired of being lied to." Tyeisha replied with a straight face.

I miss Tyeisha little bossy self. "The truth is I have no idea where your father is. I went to take care of some business. When I returned your father was gone."

"Just like that, dad was gone? Have you tried to call him? What if dad is dead?" Li l Ty became worried. That was what I was afraid of.

"Please calm down your father isn't dead. I know for a fact that he's pretty much alive. Your father was planning on leaving me. Hopefully he contacts us soon."

"Well I'm happy that he's gone. I hate him anyway." Tyeisha said.

I gasped, "Tyeisha don't say that you hate your father. Why do you hate him?" I hugged her tightly.

"He changed our lives momma. He messed everything up. I miss my baby brother Tyshawn and pretty soon we're going to get killed too." Tyeisha cried in my arms.

Big Momma walked into the room. She was standing behind the door listening to it all. "No one is going to get killed or hurt." She hugged Tyeisha and Lil Ty. "My precious grandchildren will you like to go to the grocery store with me?"

"Yes Big Momma. Can we get some taffy apples and hot crunchy cheese curls?" Lil Ty was excited. He loved going to grocery store with Big Momma. She allowed her grandchildren to get one snack of their choice.

"Whatever you want. Why don't you go downstairs and wait for me. I'll be down in a minute."

Big Momma kissed Tyeisha on the forehead before her and Lil Ty went downstairs. Now that she was alone with Emani it was time for their talk. "Emani I suggest that you get some counseling for them children. Tyeisha has been wetting the bed at night. Lil Ty is fascinated about guns. You know that I believe in a higher power but there is nothing wrong with receiving professional help."

My eyes began to water. My life was falling apart right before my eyes. Big Momma got up to leave for the store. "Wait, let me give you some money." I got up to retrieve some money from my bag giving Big Momma one thousand dollars."

"Emani you don't have to give me any money. God has blessed your grandmother with food stamps."

We both began to laugh. Big Momma always knew how to cheer me up. I loved her so much. "Take the money, it's plenty of more from where that came from."

"Emani you'll be fine, God still hasn't turned his back on you. He removes people out of your life for a reason." She left to go to the store.

I knew that she was speaking of Tyrese leaving me and the children. You know what's crazy if Tyrese was to walk through Big Momma's door right now I'll take him back. That nigga had my mind and head gone.

Chapter 24

Tavion

The birds were chirping when I arrived home. My head was banging due a tension headache. Tichina was sleeping peacefully in our California king sized bed. The only thing that I needed right now was a shower and rest. Thoughts of retiring invaded my head as the water poured down on me. I've been in the game since the age of fifteen. There was no reason to continue to risk losing everything. Money wasn't a problem. All of my businesses were bringing in great profits. The water hit my back easing some of my tension. Life changing decisions needed to be dealt with. I had so much weight on my soldiers. I stepped out of the shower wrapping the towel around my waist. Water was still dripping from my body as I sat on the edge of the bed softly not wanting to wake my queen. It was too late for that. Tichina rubbed my back gently till she reached my shoulders.

"I'm sorry baby I didn't mean to wake you." I apologized but Tichina shhhh me.

Taking her time she removed her robe exposing her perky breast. My dick raised, I was ready to take her sexy ass down. It's been a minute since I've had some of her good pussy. Looking into her eyes I could see that she wanted me as badly as I wanted her. Tichina pushed down onto the bed straddling me. When my dick slipped inside of her it felt like heaven. She bounced up and down on my dick taking control. Her super wet pussy was about to make me nut.

"Ohhhhh shit you about to make me nut bae." I told her.

"Mmmm, don't you dare nut on me right now." Tichina moaned.

"Ohhhhhhhhhhh!" My nut shot inside her wet pussy.

Tichina planted kisses on my chest working her way down. She took my limp dick into her mouth sucking and slurping on it. Her tongue tricks made my dick stand back up. My baby did her thing stuffing my dick down her throat. I grabbed a handful of her hair as she deep throated my dick. Knowing that she needed to cum; I took control turning her thick yellow ass around. She backed all her ass up on my dick throwing her ass back.

"Throw that ass back baby." I smacked her on the ass.

Tichina moaned, demanding that I go deeper and faster. I did what she requested stroking deeper and faster. Her pussy gripped my dick as she shook uncontrollable.

"Teeeeeee!" Tichina screamed my name out as she came hard. I slid my dick out of her pussy. Her cum was thick and white.

She drained the little energy that I had in me causing me to pass out.

The aroma of food awakened me. Taking a look at my phone, it was 4:47pm. *Damn did I sleep the day away?* I slipped on some boxers and jumped out of bed to brush my teeth. My stomach followed the smell of the food.

"Looks like someone has finally gotten up." Tichina turned giving me a kiss.

She was wearing a tank top and stretch shorts exposing her booty cheeks. She backed her ass up on me as she bent over to take the chicken out of the oven. My harden dick stabbed her threw my boxers.

"Why didn't you wake me up baby?" I smacked her on the ass. "What all did you cook? You got it smelling real good in here."

"I didn't wake you up because you needed your rest. I'm making baked chicken, Greens, Yams, Macaroni and Cheese and cornbread." She smiled.

"Alright I see you back to normal being a good girlfriend." I laughed.

It hit me that I left my cellphone upstairs. I ran back up to grab it. When I returned back to the kitchen Tichina was preparing my plate. I took a seat at the table going through my phone checking out my missed calls. Kenya called me, according to the call log it showed that her call was accepting. What did she and Tichina talk about for five minutes? I looked up away from my phone. Tichina made eye contact with me when she placed my plate in front of me.

"Before you starting thinking crazy, I spoke to Kenya when she called." She starting preparing her plate. I could sense that she was nervous because she dropped the serving fork.

After she was done preparing her plate Tichina said grace. Sitting across from me she stared at me weirdly waiting on me to respond back.

"So what did you and Kenya talk about for five minutes?" I questioned her.

"Nothing much. I told her that you were sleeping. Asked how she was doing. She seems pretty cool Tavion. I can't wait to meet her." Tichina smiled before stuffing her mouth with Greens.

"I'm happy that you two were able to talk. Why the sudden change on the way that you feel about her? Two days ago we were fighting about Kenya."

"Yes we were fighting about her and when you were on the road I had time to think. I was being immature and insecure over nothing. If she's a friend of yours, she's a friend of mine."

"Tichina you to have to be fake nice to Kenya on behalf of me. Kenya is a very intelligent woman, trust me she will pick up on the phoniness."

"I'm not being fake or phony when it comes to her. Tavion I trust that you love me and that Kenya's a thing of the past. How's your food bae?"

"The food is good baby. You did an excellent job." I told her ending the Kenya conversation.

Tichina was back to normal. Being a great woman to me, cooking and sexing me. It didn't matter if she fucked with Kenya or not. I was still going to look out for her by making sure that she was back on her feet. What I wasn't going to do was put her first or before Tichina. Next week Kenya will be home. I have everything set up for her. Making sure that she has a home, car and money. Kenya was my old thang that I didn't want back. It was only right that I looked out for her for doing my bid and not snitching.

The only thing that I feel comfortable with was Tichina answering my phone. If it was another caller she would've answered. Will she answer Kenya's call every time when I'm sleep? Will she get paranoid when Kenya calls me once she's out? I guess I will find out when she's released. The reminder of the evening was peaceful. Only important outbound and inbound calls were accepted. I called to check on my grandmother, she was doing fine. My people in Georgia was still working on catching up with Tyrese. After I done talking to Keith, Dee and checking on my money. All my attention was focused on Tichina. We spent the rest of the day role playing and fucking.

Chapter 25

Tyrese

"Wake up, time for you to go baby girl." I shook the pretty young thang that was laying in my bed. She was a thick ass girl who I met at the bar downstairs in the hotel.

She rolled over still looking gorgeous as last night. "Ty why can't I stay a little longer." She grabbed my hard dick.

I pushed her face down toward my dick. Baby girl took care of my dick as I lit up my blunt. Puffing on the blunt I blew smoke circles in the air as I thought about Emani. Deep down inside I felt guilty about leaving her. At the last minute I felt that Emani was going to slow me down here in Georgia. She was beginning to become a distraction and I needed to focus on making money here. As soon I get on my feet, I'll send for her and my children. Baby girl continued to suck my soul out of me. Five minutes later she was swallowing my nut. She took my blunt out of my hand and hit it.

"Can I stay a little longer?" She smiled slying.

I took a look at her. Maybe keeping her around wasn't a bad idea. She was from here and could show me around Georgia. "Yes you can beautiful. What's your name? Tell me more about you."

"You had to be drunk last night because I told you that my name is Savannah," she giggled. "I'm twenty five years old, no children and a model. I can't believe that you were that wasted from last night."

"I had to be because I don't remember none of that shit. You cool and can hang around for a little while. All I ask is that you do what I say and just look beautiful."

"That's not a problem as long as I'm being compensated." Savannah licked her lips.

"Modeling is the new cover up for selling pussy now." I chuckled.

"Call it what you want to call it. I'm good at what I do and expect to be compensated for it. If not I can go on my way. It's your choice."

Savannah little hoe ass wasn't lying about being good at what she does. I didn't remember her name last night. One thing that I did remember was her pussy. At the end of the day she wasn't anything but a prostitute. She was beautiful, perfect tight body and could be an asset to me if I could get in her head.

"How much we talking?" I asked her.

Savannah smiled as she rolled over onto her back. "I just want a Chanel bag a pair of sneakers."

"That little pussy expensive." I got up to shower. I had shit to do today.

"My little pussy is worth it." Savannah stood at the bathroom door. "You're not going to invite me to get in the shower with you?"

"For a pair of Chanel sneakers and purse I shouldn't have to tell you. Your ass should be in here washing me down."

Savannah did what she was told without talking back. This little bitch would be good to train and to send off. I wasn't big on tricking off, this would be the last time I broke bread on this hoe. We both got dressed. The first stop was the mall. She jumped in the car with me explaining that she took an Uber to the hotel.

"Do you like to hang out at hotel bars?" I questioned her.

"Only that one. My friend bartends there so I get drinks on the house." Savannah replied.

At the mall I bought me a few items and what she asked for. As much money that I already spent on her I really didn't want to feed the bitch. Savannah was happy when I pulled into The Capital Grille parking lot. She acted as if she never been to a fancy restaurant before. When the waitress sat us her eyes lit up.

"Excuse me while I go to the washroom," she got up. I watched her thick ass as she walked away. She turned a few of the men heads in the restaurant too.

While she was in the washroom I made a phone call to my cousin who lived here. She was in the music industry. Currently she was there on business. My cousin couldn't talk long but told me that she will be back tonight. First thing in the morning she would get up with me. Savannah returned back to the table. We placed our orders and got better acquainted with each other. She talked on and on about her modeling career. Sipping on my drink I watched her adding up the dollar signs in heads. All I could think about is how much that she could make me.

Interrupting her I asked, "Savannah is modeling paying the bills?"

"Not really, it's up and down. I just need a big break. Like being in a video dancing next to Drake or Rick Ross." She smiled.

"Sounds like you need a manager. I have a cousin who's in the music industry with a lot of major artist. I can make things happen for you."

"I'm very interested in being managed. Do you think that I have what it takes to be the next hot video vixen?"

Savannah stood up so that I could admire her sexy body. She was bad than a mother fucker. Perfect clear caramel skin tone. High cheekbones, short, small waist with wide hips and ass for days. I had the money to clean her up and to make things happen. First I had to get my shit together. That was finding a place to stay.

"Yes you have what it takes beautiful. Where do you live?"

Savannah smiled taking a seat. "I live not too far from the hotel. About twenty minutes away with my roommate. I really don't have a room." She lowered her eyes, "I sleep on the couch. It's not too bad because I'm rarely there."

I lifted her chin up. "You never have to go back. You can stay with me."

"Thank you Ty, I was hoping that you would take me in. Does this mean that I'm your woman now?" she blushed.

Before I answered that I thought about Emani. I made a promise to her that once we relocated to Georgia that I would stop being the old Tyrese. "Nah baby girl, only my client with benefits."

"I'm cool with that," she licked her lips smiling.

Our food arrived, we ate and discussed more about the plans I had for her. We wrapped it up and left. On the way home we made a stop at the liquor store. I sent Savannah inside to buy a fifth of 1738 and blunts. Since my cousin and I wasn't going to conduct business until tomorrow, it was best if we just relaxed in the room. Savannah grabbed the empty ice bucket.

"Baby I'm going to get some ice." She swayed out of the room.

I rolled up the weed and searched for something funny to watch. Friday was on, Smokey was taking a shit on the side of the house. I hit the blunt laughing at his ass. She returned back to the room. As I smoked she made our drinks, passing me my glass while she undressed. We were both sipping and smoking laughing at the movie. My head started pounding and the room started spinning. My glass of 1738 hit the carpet spilling everywhere.

"What the fuck is going on?" I tried to get up but fell back down.

Savannah hit the blunt laughing viciously. She straddled on top of me. "How you feeling Ty?" she kissed me. **Punch!** I hit her, not as hard as I wanted to. The spiked drink was taking over. Savannah punched me in the face. "Ty it was so much fun hanging out with you, but now it's time to go." She pulled out her Beretta attaching the silencer on.

"Who sent you hoe?" I slurred.

Savannah screwed the silencer onto the gun. She aimed the gun to my temple shooting me twice in the head. Before leaving she checked Ty's pulse making sure that he was dead. "Who's the hoe now?" she snickered. She took her drinking glass, cleaned the room and got dressed. "Stupid mother fucker." She mumbled as she took the bag of cash that belonged to Tyrese. That was an additional bonus along with the Chanel sneakers and bag. When she received the call from Tavion she no problem doing the job for him. Savannah was Kenya's younger cousin who moved from Illinois to Georgia three years ago. She was college student by day and bartender by night. Her beauty and charm always made a nigga weak. Savannah exited the hotel walking a block to her parked car. Once she got behind the wheel she made a phone call, "Hello it's done."

Chapter 26

Kamara

Transitioning to change was easy for Karlie and I. Karlie was reading me a story while I relaxed on new plush sofa. Keith was out making runs. Now that I was pregnant my appetite grew twice as much.

"Karlie your reading is getting much better." I encouraged my baby girl. Academically she was exceeding in reading but not doing as greater in math. "Enough for today, tomorrow we will work on your math."

Karlie frowned up, "Momma I hate math. Why can't I just read forever? Do I have to learn math?" she whined.

"Yes you do, math is just as important as reading. Think about when you're at the candy store buying junk food. You have to count your money to pay them. You have to make sure that they don't cheat you out of your money." I explained to her.

"Okay momma I will practice my math tomorrow." Karlie went from frowning to smiling, "Momma can I write a book when I'm older?" she asked.

"Sure baby girl. As a matter of fact you can write a book at your age. With me to assist you."

Karlie happily jumped up and down. "Momma can I start tomorrow?"

Karlie gave me a big hug. At that moment Keith walked in carrying groceries. I walked Karlie upstairs to her bedroom, turning on a cartoon movie. When I made it back downstairs to the kitchen, Keith was carrying in the last of the groceries. He took off his shirt wearing a white wife beater exposing his muscles. *"Calm down kitty cat"* I told myself. A smile grew up my face as I went through the grocery bags. I see that he purchased all my snacks. My pregnant ass was ready to slam. The first thing that I grabbed was the big jar of pickles.

Keith took it out of my hands, "Allow your King to open this up for you." He popped open the jar of pickles.

"Thank you King." Taking a fork I picked the biggest pickle out of the jar. "This big one will do." I replied before taking a bite of it.

"I got a bigger pickle for you." Keith laughed.

"You're so nasty that's why I love you." We both kissed,

I tried to help Keith put away the food but he told that he got it. So I took a seat at the kitchen table eating my pickle. Keith was such a good man. He's everything thing I wanted in a man. The day that Tavion introduced us I felt that he was going to be the one. I like to think of him as my knight in shining armor. He came just in time after dealing with Karlie's father. I was damaged goods and emotionally drained. Keith helped me with that, standing by my side as I healed. And still loving me through my pain and scars. He could've chosen another women to be with. One with less baggage. Instead he wanted me and accepted my daughter as well. It felt great to finally be in a much better environment. One that wasn't filled with domestic abuse. I fell in love the moment that I took my first step into his home. Now it was our home. Keith made sure that most of my and Karlie things were brought from my home to here. Explaining to Karlie wasn't hard to do. Keith and I sat her down and explained to her that moving in a bigger home is much better. Never telling her about the gruesome details that occurred at our old home. I was able to place my home on the market for sale. There was no way that I was staying there anymore. Some nights I was still having nightmares of Keith killing the hit woman. He would hold me tight rocking me back to sleep. For the last two nights I haven't had a nightmare. This evening Keith and I are going to talk have a talk to Karlie about the baby.

"What would you like me to cook tonight?" I asked my loving man.

"Baby whatever you cook is fine with me. You know that I love your cooking."

He hugged me from behind kissing the side of my neck. Keith loved seafood, so that's what it'll be for tonight. I defrosted the salmon and took out my sides. Keith went in the family room to watch a baseball game. He was such a sports fanatic. While I sat in the kitchen, I logged onto my Facebook account. Keith told me to deactivate my page last week but I secretly kept it. There wasn't much going on. The same old bullshit of bitches who were fake rich and famous. Niggas who were the new bitches. Posting more pictures than the hoes. Social media has turned into strictly entertainment and a circus. All these wack as people were pretending to be someone that they weren't. Thank goodness that I've never been the type to want to impress others. I continued to scroll down my timeline when something caught my eye. I'm Facebook friends with Emani children. I know that their too young for pages but hey they have one. Anyway, her daughter Tyeisha posted a picture caption, "We're Back Together Again". It was a picture of her catching Emani off guard sitting in a chair while her and Lil Ty laughing about something. Before jumping to conclusions I checked for details that would tell me how updated this picture is. Emani, Tyeisha and Lil Ty were wearing the new Jordan's that just came out. The reason why I knew that they just dropped was because Keith purchased him and Karlie a pair. Emani was back in town without a care doing her old bullshit. Splurging and spending money on her and them damn children. I grew livid that she was back like nothing never happened. Angrily I went to inform Keith.

"What's up bae? Why you frowned up?" he sat up lowering the foot rest of his Lazy Boy chair.

I pushed my cellphone in his face. "Take a look at this."

Keith stared at the phone, taking his time to read the caption. He looked up at me, "Get the fuck out of here." He jumped up to get his phone that was on the coffee table and made a call.

That dirty bitch had some nerve to even show her face around here after all that she caused. Now I was confused, if she was here Ty had to be with her. Keith was on the phone talking to either Tavion or Dee. I'm not sure which partner it was. I sat on the couch rocking back and forth, the hate that I had inside of me against her grew ten times worst. I waited for Keith to end his call before I spoke.

"I didn't think that bitch was that dumb to go back to Big Momma's house. If she is there Tyrese isn't too far behind." I said.

"Nah, Tyrese isn't there because he's dead." Keith gave a nonchalant shrug.

"Wait, I thought you said that you couldn't find him? Unless something changed within the last forty eight hours."

Keith gave me a look that assured that Tyrese was indeed dead. That's the best news that I've heard all mother fucking day. True when Tootie was killed that was all good as well. Tootie deserved that death. Hell she betrayed all of them on her team and flipped right on Tyrese dick. Now it was time for us to start planning Emani's death.

"Baby we get shit done. We don't do no fucking around. I see Emani think that this is a fucking game." Keith said.

I knew that I was fucking with a real killer. A soft part formed in my heart when I looked back at the picture. Tyeisha and Lil Ty were so happy to be reunited back with their mom. It hurt me because all of that was going to come to end.

"Give me your phone." Keith held out his right hand waiting on me to handle him my phone.

I pouted my lips giving him my sad eyes. "Don't give me that sad puppy dog look. Give me the phone." He laughed.

"I have a solution, hear me out. You know that I've known Emani for years. Why don't we use my approach? I can call her up and get her to meet up with me."

"You sure that she'll meet up with you Kamara? The last time that she tried to reconnect with you it didn't go as planned."

"I'm more than sure that she would meet up with me."

Keith took out his phone to call Tavion to see if he was up with the plan. He didn't have a problem with it. Dee actually thought that it was a wise idea as well. Before I called her I had to come up with a plan.

Chapter 27

Emani

For the last two days I've been spending more time with my children. With some of the money I rented a three bedroom apartment up North on Wellington Avenue and Central. It was in a place where not many people would be able to bump into me. Living with Big Momma in one bedroom wasn't the best option for me to lay my head. I was an easy target, close for them to get to menthe cute cozy three bedroom apartment wasn't as big as our home that we loss. My children didn't care about that, they were so happy that we were all back together. I purchased furniture, not the top of the line. Just something basic nothing fancy like in my old home. We all settled down at our four seat kitchen table eating dinner. For once in my life it was peaceful with Tyrese not being around. The three of us were laughing and discussing the latest children topics. It felt good to catch up with them.

"Mom I miss you're cooking." Tyeisha talked with her mouth full of my tasty mashed potatoes.

"Baby don't eat with your mouth full." I laughed.

After dinner Tyeisha helped me wash and dry the dishes. It was getting close to bedtime, they both showered and went to bed. Finally it was time for me to shower and lay down. I oiled up my body and laid down. My room was dark without a television. No matter how much destruction Tyrese brought into my life, I missed him. I haven't had any dick in weeks. It was hard for me to go without fucking when I used to getting fucked every day. Thoughts of Tyrese fucking me clouded in my head. Gently I rubbed my clit. My pussy was screaming for attention. In my nightstand my brand new bullet and AA batteries was waiting on me. Not too far from my house there was a sex store that I bought it from. It wasn't a dick but it will do the job. I inserted the batteries into my pink bullet. The vibration was powerful as I set it on the highest setting. Shit this little bitch strong. I rubbed my nipples as I kept the vibrating bullet on my clit. I imagined the biggest dick that I ever had. That dick belonged to Jay. Even though we only fucked once, that one time he fucked the shit out of me. I fantasied about how Jay hit my pussy from the side and back.

"Ohhhhh Jay, fuck me real good." I moaned. The bullet made me climax instantly. My body jerked as I had the first orgasm with a toy. I crossed my legs, rolled on my right side and dozed off to sleep.

***

Ring! Ring! Ring! The nonstop ringing of my cellphone woke me. There was number across the screen that I didn't recognize. "Hello." I answered.

"Hey Emani this is Tyrese's Cousin Joy from Atlanta," she sniffed. Joy was Tyrese first cousin on his father side. His father side of the family lived in Atlanta. That's why Ty wanted to relocate there.

The sounds of sniffles was a hint that it was bad news. "What's going on Joy?"

"I regret to inform you that Tyrese is dead. He was found shot in the head twice inside his hotel room." Joy cried into the phone.

I felt a part of me leaving my body. "Nooooo!" I yelled, crying hysterically. "This can't be true, please tell me that you're lying."

"It's all true Emani. Do you think that you could get down here as soon as possible?" Joy asked.

Suddenly my heart felt with anger and revenge. "Get down there for what?! Fuck him! He left his children and me! Yall got me fucked up if you think that I'm coming to see about him!" I was beyond angry.

"Emani fuck you and them children you selfish bitch! Now I understand why he left your ass!" Joy spat.

"Bitch I don't give a fuck about him, you or yall fake ass family. Yall can cremate that dirty nigga for all I care!"

I pressed the button on the phone ending the call. "Fuck! Fuck! Fuck!" I cried throwing shit around in my bedroom. My children ran into the room "Ma what's going on?" Tyeisha grabbed my arms stopping me from throwing things. I cried into my daughter arms, "Your father is dead."

Tyeisha didn't say anything she just rubbed my back. Lil Ty stood at the door watching us looking sadly. He walked over sitting next to us on the bed. "Good he's dead." Lil Ty replied dryly.

***

Hearing the news about Tyrese death made me one hundred and fifty thousand richer. That's right, I had a nice insurance policy on his trifling ass. All along while he was plotting against me. I was two steps ahead, plotting on him. What I told his cousin Joy I meant every word of it. Fuck Tyrese he could burn. Ashes to ashes, dust to fuck niggas. I called up my insurance agent and did the necessary steps to collect my money. Today I was in the mood to shop. First thing that I did was drop of my children to Big Momma's house. When I arrived, Big Momma was sitting on her porch. The raggedy bible that she had for years sat in her lap. My children gave their grandmother a hug before entering her home.

"How you doing baby?" Big Momma asked me with sincerity in her eyes.

I gave her a big hug, "Not too good. Tyrese was killed. Shot in the head twice in Atlanta."

Big Momma took hold to my hands. "Oh lawd Emani. I'm sorry to hear that. Are you going to Atlanta to see about him?"

"No I'm not Big Momma." She looked at me with sadness in her eyes. "Please don't try to talk me out of either." I turned my head away. Her hypnotizing eyes weren't going to work on me. She turned my face back toward her. "I can't make you do anything because you're grown. If you don't want to go, you don't have to."

For the first time in my life, Big Momma didn't preach to me. Instead she held onto my hand and supported my decision. "You do what's best for you and your children. Their all you got now Emani." Big Momma replied.

Tears streamed down my face. The man that I loved and cherished since my teenager years was gone. Everything that we built was gone. All the dreams that we shared was never going to happen.

"Big Momma I can't stand to lose another person. First Tyshawn, now Tyrese… I can't… I can't." I cried.

Big Momma held me as we sat on the porch like she used to do when I was younger. The sound of my mom's voice could be heard. My mom Boogie, that's what the streets called her was loudly talking to someone from across the street. A stray black cat walked ahead of her as she made her way over to the porch.

"Look what the cat dragged this way." I mumbled under my breath. Boogie looked as if she was high as hell.

"Hey my beautiful daughter." Tightly hugging me, squeezing the air out of me. For a fact I knew that she was high. Boogie has never been this nice to me. "What's going on? Why you look like you've been crying?"

"Tyrese was killed Ma."

Boogie bent down and whispered in my ear so that Big Momma didn't hear her, "Good I always hated his ass."

That was my exit to leave before I act a fool in front of Big Momma. "Big Momma I'm about to make some runs. I gave my children some money so that they could order some food when they got hungry." I stood up dusting the dirt off my bottom.

"Where you going, can I tag along?" Boogie asked.

"No you can't because you like to shoplift." I told her.

"Looks whose talking the apple doesn't fall to far from the tree. Besides I have money." Boogie out a wad of cash from her bra. I don't even care how she earned. Don't ask, don't tell was my motto.

"Sure you can go, but if you get caught stealing I'm leaving you where you at." I gave Big Momma a kiss. "I won't be long and I'll bring you something back."

"You two be careful out in them streets." Big Momma told us both.

Me and mother left, still I couldn't believe that I was allowing her to go with me. The destination was Michigan Avenue. On the ride to downtown my mother and I sang every song on the radio together. We were actually vibing, not fighting. Over the years we had a bad falling out about her drug habit. Boogie felt that Ty was to give her breaks because she was family. That's where her and Tyrese bumped heads at. They both had a blowout with me caught in the middle. My mother carried bitter feelings of resentment toward me. Our relationship as mother and daughter has never been the same. Thankfully we made it to the Watertower without any arguments.

"Ma I'm going to shop. Meet me back at the food court in two hours." I held up two fingers to show her that I meant two hours or else her ass was getting left.

"Alright see you in two hours." Boogie walked off.

My first stop was Macy's. I was in need of a new wardrobe. Starting over from scratch because I loss a lot of my clothing back at my house. There was no need for me to check price tags. Money wasn't a problem because my insurance check will be clearing soon. With that type of money and the money that I have put up I could leave Illinois. My children and I could move to Minnesota and I can find them a white step daddy. I picked out several pair of jeans and proceeding to the dressing room to try each of them on. While I was hopping in my second pair of jeans, I received an incoming call.

Ring! Ring! Ring! I searched inside my Louie bag for my phone. On the fourth ring I answered, "Hello."

"Hey Emani what's going on? This is Kamara." I looked at my phone oddly.

"Kamara I know your voice. Ain't shit going on, what you doing calling me?"

"Despite all the bullshit that's going I still care about my God children. I was calling to see how they were doing." Kamara replied.

"How did you get my new number?" I questioned her.

"I saw Boogie on Chicago Avenue and Leclaire asked her for your number and she gave it to me." Kamara said.

"This is funny how you're trying to connect with me now. Being that the last time we met up you were ready to knock my head off. Now all of a sudden you're concerned about my damn children?"

"Emani my God children don't have shit to do with this. You know what, forget that I even placed this call." Kamara was second from hanging up.

"Kamara wait, Lil Ty and Tyeisha are doing fine. How is my Karlie doing? They really miss you both a lot and talk about you all the time." I lied.

"Good to know that their doing well. Karlie is being Karlie, you know." Both of or phony asses laughed.

"Thanks for calling to check on them. I'll be sure to let them know that you called." *Click!*

Receiving that phone call was strange to me. Fuck trying on these jeans. It was time for me to get the fuck out of here. For all I know they could be watching me right now. I rushed out of the dressing room nearly knocking the sales woman down.

I hit up Boogie, "Ma we have to go. Meet me in front of Starbucks in five minutes. "I made it to Starbucks waiting on my mother. Five minutes had gone by. *"Where the fuck is Boogie?"* I thought. I called her again, this time she didn't answer. *"Five more minutes, if she's not here I'm leaving the bitch!"* Three minutes later, Boogie arrived. She strolled over to me while talking on her cellphone and carrying Forever 21 bags. "Let's go please!" I snatched her by the arm walking quickly out of there.

Boogie placed her phone inside her bra. "Damn, you don't have to snatch me up." She snatched her right arm away following behind me.

Not wanting to cause a scene I remained quiet all the way to the car. Once we got inside I chewed her ass up. "If I tell you to meet me ASAP that's what the fuck I mean!"

"Girl you better watch your mouth. I still am your mom and will fuck you up." Boogie tried to get tough. "Why are you rushing anyway?" she asked.

"Kamara just called me out of the blue. Who in the fuck told you to give her my number?" I jumped lane to lane. These people downtown didn't know how to drive. "Something wasn't right about that phone call."

"Emani yall been friends forever, so what I gave her your number." Boogie nonchalantly replied. She received a text from someone smiling into the phone. "Drop me off at MacArthur's to meet my man up there. We're about to sit down and eat." She smiled.

"You have a man?" I laughed thinking to myself, *more like a getting high buddy.*

Punching the gas, I hit the expressway going 60 mph flying past all the drivers that wanted to do the speed limit today. I exited off Laramie taking it up to Madison. Everyone was outside the young and old hoes, the pack workers and people who really had a reason to be out. As I drove down Madison, Boogie continued to text her getting high buddy. I parked in front of the restaurant.

"Alright ma, get out." I didn't care about being rude. Boogie was moving slowly. "Why you are moving so damn slow when you know that I'm in a rush?!"

"Emani wait! Damn, someone wants to talk to you." Boogie said.

"It's not a good time for me to meet your boyfriend ma."

Boogie paid me no mind. Her attention was ahead, that's when I noticed Kamara getting out of her car walking toward me. "Ma you foul as fuck for having her meet me up here!"

"Girl just talk to her that's your childhood friend. What bad could come out of it?" Boogie shady ass replied.

I looked around checking my mirrors. Fuck! Dee was trying to pull up behind me. He had a grimaced look upon his face. That's when I realized that Boogie set me up. I punched on the gas and tried to ride of. Kamara jumped in front of my car pounding on my hood, "Emani you can't run forever!" she yelled.

"Move bitch!" Kamara didn't move. I punched on the gas…… **Vroommmm**! Kamara fell to the ground. I flew down Madison Street with Dee on my ass a few cars behind me. "Look what the fuck you got me in! You sold your own daughter out for a little money!" I yelled at my mother. **Pop**! **Crack**! Dee shot my back window out.

Boogie started screaming hysterically. **Pop**! My mother's body slumped forward. Blood was pouring out the back of her head. Dee was on my ass. Luckily for me the shoots were hitting in my car. Other cars scattered out of the way. When I made it Madison and Parkside my tires were blown out. 15th District Police station was one block away. *Please God let me make it to the police station."* **Pop! Pop! Pop!** I was hit in the shoulder. **Boom**! I crashed into a parked car. "Fuck!" I dipped out of the car running down Madison running inside the police station. The police officers pulled their guns out aiming at me.

"Please don't shoot me! Someone is trying to kill me! I've been shot!" I collapsed on the floor in pain.

A female officer rushed over to me. "She's losing a lot of blood," she yelled. Quickly another officer took off his shirt giving it to her. The female officer applied pressure on the right side of my stomach. That's when I found out that I was shot there.

The pain was unbearable. "Please don't let me die." I cried to the female officer.

"Hang in there, the paramedics are on the way."

Chapter 28

Kamara

The paramedics rushed me to West Suburban Hospital since that was the closest to me. I notified Keith letting him know what happened. He was furious and on his way to the hospital. I was in pain. Emani hit me and ran over my foot. It didn't take long for me to get there. The doctor and nurses rushed me to the back. They gave me an ultrasound making sure that my fetus and placenta was fine. Keith arrived when I was getting my ultrasound. He sat in the room until they returned me back to the emergency room. The look on Keith's face showed how mad that he was.

"I didn't think that it will happen like that." I tried to explain to Keith.

"Kamara I told you that meeting up with Emani was a bad idea."

"You did say that, from here on out I will listen to you. Good thing is the baby is fine. By foot is going to be fine too." I tried to ease the tension.

"I'm happy that you and our baby is fine. Now we have to worry about Emani. I got word that she was air lifted to Loyola Hospital. That bitch better die because if she doesn't I'm going to kill that bitch personally." Keith meant what he said.

"Keith I don't want to get your hands dirty. If I lose you to a murder case then I'll have to raise two children alone. Emani will get what's coming to her."

The doctor walked inside with my chart in his hand. "Great news Kamara your baby is fine. However we will have to keep you overnight for observation."

"I'm very happy to hear that. I wish that I could take something stronger for pain." I whined.

"Sorry, acetaminophen is the only thing that I will give you. In a few days. I could have the nurse place a cold compress on your foot." The doctor explained.

"Anything that will help with the pain is fine with me."

The ER doctor wrote somethings in my chart before leaving. Keith took out his phone to call Tavion. He took Karlie to their place so that Tichina could watch her. Both Tichina and Tavion was cool with the arrangements. The transporter wheeled me to the observation unit. In the room there was a couch you can lounge on. Keith made himself comfortable on the couch.

I broke the quietness in the room. "Thank you for loving me. Since day one I've been a handful. You know with my baby daddy problems, him damn near killing me and now this. I'm such a handful"

"You don't have to thank me for loving you. If anything I should be thanking you. I'm the one that's in the streets. You dealing with a man like me is new to you. I'm a target that has to be stressful for you to deal with. I know that you worried about me." Keith opened up about his feelings.

"You have no idea how much that I worry about losing you. Then I get pregnant, that wasn't a part of the plan. Not only that, Karlie and I moved in with you. Keith I feel like a charity case."

"Charity case? You're my woman, what's mines is yours. You're smart, beautiful and an excellent mom. You're great with numbers. You can go back to school to get a degree in whatever you want. I'll pay for it, you know money isn't a problem. You can open up a business, whatever you want to do. I have your back."

Keith and I continued our serious talk. This was the first time that we really opened up about everything. My emotions were all over the place. I don't know if it was the hormones from the baby or not. Maybe it was that I wanted Keith out of the damn streets. I was serious about being a charity case. I had to get back to doing something. Make myself productive. Starting my own business didn't sound bad at all. Keith was right about having money. We were financially stable, but fuck the money. My children need a man in their lives to raise them.

***

In the middle of the night I woke up. Keith was laid out on the small couch knocked out. My mouth was dry, but under doctors order I was NPO *couldn't have anything to drink or eat.* Quietly I got up to go to the bathroom, not wanting to disturb Keith. After I washed my hands I sneaked a sip of water. Before laying back down I walked over kissing Keith gently on the cheek. It felt good loving somebody, when somebody loves you back.

Chapter 29

Dee

It was time to do things my way and take it to another level. Tory and I parked in the cut behind Big Momma's house. There wasn't a person in sight which made it easier for what we were about to do. We both loaded our glocks as we crept up the four wooden stairs. The back door was flimsy, easy to break in. We entered inside peeping the scene making sure the coast was clear. The first floor was clean, not a person in sight. Voices could be heard from upstairs.

"This way." I nodded my head in the direction up the steps. Step by step we went quietly until we reached the bedrooms. The first bedroom was empty. The second bedroom was where all the action was. We barged inside a room full of children. They all turned to look at us in surprise.

"Help! Help!" they all screamed. Damn this was going to harder than I thought. One of the shorties ran up kicking me between the legs. "You little fucker!" I grabbed him by the neck throwing him into the wall. He fell down onto the floor crying. Tory grabbed Tyeisha and Lil Ty dragging them out of the room. "Let me go!" Lil Ty punched Tory but it didn't faze him. They both put up a fight till we made it to the car. The windows on the Impala was heavy tinted so no one was going to be able to see them. "Where are you taking us?" Tyeisha asked us. We both ignored her driving to our next location.

We arrived at our honeycomb hideout with two sleeping children in the back seat. One of my solders carried them both inside the house. It was a room in the back for them with two beds, no television or windows. They both woke up from all the moving around. "Please don't hurt us." Tyeisha cried. Oh how I wish that I could promise them that I wouldn't do that.

"That's up to your mom." I told them. They both looked afraid when I check their pockets for gadgets and cellphones. They both were clean with nothing on them. "Are you hungry?" I asked them.

"Yes." Tyeisha replied. Lil Ty never said a word, he just looked at me like he wanted to kill me.

I left out of the room, giving my soldiers strict instructions. "Go buy them some wings and something to drink. Always keep the door lock and someone here to watch them. When they go to the bathroom you must watch and wait for them outside the door. Under no circumstances are you to harm them. If they become a problem call me."

"We got it Dee." They told me.

I knew that they weren't going to fuck up. I wasn't worried about anyone hearing them because their room was sound proof. If Emani wanted to see her children alive, she'll cooperate. If not they were going to die.

***

When I made it home to my surprise my loving Dasia was still up. She was sitting up in our King sized bed. "What's up baby? Did the twins keep you up" I asked her.

Dasia didn't say a word. She turned on the television, the news was on. The news reporter covered Emani's shooting. I took a look while taking a seat on the edge of the bed.

"Why did I have to find out from Tichina that you were taking care of business?" she questioned me.

"Baby I was going to tell you. I'm sorry that I didn't, it won't happen again." I tried to explain.

"Dustin I've been calling your phone worried about you. You've never not answered for me."

I undressed removing my shirt and jeans. "Dasia my apologies for not answering your calls." I gave her a kiss.

Dasia adjusted her attitude, "So what's the plan because the bitch is still alive? Dee you better pray that she doesn't snitch. You killed her mom, that's deep."

"Trust me baby she won't talk. I took care of that. As far as her mom, she got what she deserved. Setting up your mom for a couple of dollars. The loyalty was gone a long time ago."

"Damn her own mother, that's fucked up. You better have it under control because I can't have you going to jail for life."

"Don't worry your pretty head about me. How are my twin baby girls? Did you finish writing your cookbook?"

"The twins ate and slept all day. Which was good because I was able to finish my cookbook. Would you like to take a look at it before I send it to my publisher?"

"Yes baby, but first let me shower. I promise that I won't be long."

Dasia grabbed her laptop, "Okay bae, and don't be long."

The hot water felt so damn good. For a moment I stood there allowing the water to pour over me. I was exhausted and tired of all the bullshit. My heart was hurting and filled with anger. I missed my twin brother so much. We both had plans to conquer the world. I cried in the shower releasing my steam. Emani better be thankful that I was a father now. If it wasn't for my family I would've killed her children a long time ago. In the past I've been shot and had broken bones. None of that pain compares to losing my brother.

Knock! Knock! "Babe everything is fine." I lied to Dasia.

She entered into our bathroom, "No it's not fine. I'm not going to sleep until you join me." Dasia said. I stepped out of the shower, she handed me a towel out of the warmer. "Dustin I'm going to schedule an appointment tomorrow with a therapist."

"I keep telling you that I don't need any counseling. I got everything under control." I wrapped the towel around my waist.

Dasia stood in the middle of her bedroom with her hands on her hips. "No you don't, every night you think that I don't hear you crying? Now this, you shooting and killing people again. You have to get you some help because you have me and twin daughters that are depending on you."

Dasia always soften me and kept my ass in check. She was bossy the first moment that I met her. It was at the grocery store. I spotted her in the seasoning aisle reaching for turmeric on the top shelf. Only being 4'9" she was having a hard time. I laughed and she got upset checking me with her smart ass mouth. It was the way that she checked me that turned me on. She used big words. I could tell that she was highly educated. She was beautiful. When I finally got her to smile I fell in love with her. She introduced herself, told me that she was a chef. After we talked Dasia gave me her business card. I didn't push up on her then, instead I went about it another way. When I got home that day I had Shay, Justin's woman schedule a private dinner for four at my place. Dasia came over and cooked never knowing that she was going to be a part of the small dinner. My charming ways convinced her to join us for dinner. Three years later Dasia and I are still rocking and rolling.

"Schedule the appointment." I agreed with Dasia, the last thing that I wanted to do was argue with my Queen.

She kissed me, "I'll be right by your side like I've always been, since the first day we met."

"That's why I love you. I'm blessed to have you." I tossed her little ass onto our bed.

Dasia giggled, "We're blessed to have each other. Now fuck me, we'll discuss my cookbook tomorrow." She pulled me closer to her sucking on my bottom lips. I entered her slowly, her eyes widening and then her face grimaced as I went deeper. I began to fuck her merciless as she begged for more. Dasia loved it rough, she was my freaky bitch. Her body collapsed under my weight. I held up both of her legs fucking the shit out of her ass.

"Go deeper, baby deeper." Dasia moaned. I increased my speed and went deeper knocking her pussy out. She thrusted her hips causing me to nut. I was trying to time her orgasm, knowing hers was almost there. Dasia body tensed then shook as I groaned pulling out quickly. Dasia just had the twins we weren't supposed to fucking. My thick, creamy white nut shot all over her belly. Using the towel I used to dry myself off with I cleaned the nut off her.

"I love you bae." Dasia curled up in my arms like my big baby drifting off to sleep.

***

It was 10:47am when I woke up. Dasia was feeding both of the twins. One by breast and the other with breast milk from the bottle. "Good Morning to the three ladies that I love." I got up to brush my teeth. Dasia smiled when I took Devina into my arms continuing feeding her with the bottle. The moment when I found out that we were having twins I was very excited. Dasia was nervous about it in the beginning. Feeling that two babies at once could be very overwhelming. I assured her that I would be the best father that I and my twin brother never had. Baby Devina looked at me with her piercing eyes. "You looking just like your mama." I laughed making baby talk to her. She made bubbles with her milk. "Are you full baby girl?" I laid her across my chest to burp her.

"You're getting better daddy." Dasia teased me.

"I told you that I got this." Moments later Baby Devina let out a big burp. "Little greedy self." I laughed switching babies with Dasia. Baby Devika was up next to get burped. They were both identical, at first I couldn't tell them apart. It took me two weeks, Dasia helped me out. Baby Devika had a small mole on her chin. I burped her as well, she wiggled and giggled at me. They were the joy of my life. "Now that their fed, what are we going to eat?" I asked Dasia

Dasia pulled out her cellphone. "Order from the breakfast spot that we like. I want a steak omelet, pancakes, and eggs. Hook us up bae." Dasia laid the twins down onto their blankets playing with them.

I placed an order from our favorite spot on Uber Eats. My security cameras caught me and Dasia attention. There was an unexpected visitor on our property. The small Toyota Camry pulled up in front of our home. The driver popped the trunk walking to the back to retrieve some luggage. An older woman stepped out of the back seat of the car.

Dasia eyes popped out of her eyes. "Is that my mother?" She jumped out of bed grabbing her robe to put on and running out the front door. I stayed with the twins watching everything from the security cameras. They both hugged, Dasia helped her mom with the luggage into our house.

"Where is my son and twin granddaughter of mine at?" Mama Delores yelled. I walked downstairs carrying both of the twins in my arms. "Here we are Mama Delores."

Mama Delores stood there in awe as I brought her twin granddaughters to her. Her eyes watered up as she cried tears of joy. She took a seat onto our sofa, making herself comfortable. I placed them each in her arms. "This is Devika and Devina, your grand babies." Dasia smiled with tears in her eyes.

"Oh my God, their so precious just like the pictures that you sent me." Mama Delores gazed into their eyes. The twins giggled, making baby noises. It was as if they were talking to her. "They look like the both of you. How have you two been doing?" Mama Delores asked. "I'm sorry about barging in on you so early. I know that you weren't expecting me till next week." Mama Delores leaked out the surprised.

Dasia eyes darted from me, to her mom and back at me. "You were trying to surprise me?" She laughed.

"Yes I felt that we needed help with the twins. What better person to help us out with them. Mama Delores, to the rescue." I hugged her.

"When he called me I was so happy that I couldn't wait till next week." Mama Delores smiled.

"Mama let me show you to your room and give you a tour of our home." Dasia took one of the twins from her mom as she walked her upstairs. I grabbed Mama Delores luggage following behind them.

This was Mama Delores first time being at our new home. Before she relocated from Chicago to Arizona we were living downtown. It's been two years since she's been back to Chicago. Mama Delores is Dasia sweet kind hearted mom. Dasia is her only child, she raised her by herself after Dasia's father was killed in the streets of Chicago was she ten years old. I loved her like a mom as well. When Justin and I loss our mother to cancer, she filled that void for me. Mama Delores always said that I reminded her of Dasia's father. A great man that didn't play when it came to his woman. She loved me like a son, treated me with respect and was trustworthy. Dasia bought her mom a house in Arizona. Mama Delores wanted to be there with her sister. At first Dasia didn't take it too well, but I made sure that we visited Mama Delores twice a year. Things have changed now that we have the twin girls. We all felt that it was best if Mama Delores came to visit us to be here for Dasia.

"Your home is so beautiful. It's bigger in person. Tell me how is your Southern Cookbook turning out?"

"Thank you mama. Now that you're here when can both go over the cookbook? I'm wrapping it up now. You're going to love it. I added your potato salad and dressing recipe." Dasia excitedly said as she went to go grab her laptop. I set back and watched all four of them. Dasia, Mama Delores and the twins gathered around enjoying themselves. I was so happy to bring joy and happiness into Dasia's life.

Our food arrived from Uber Eats. I offered my food to Mama Delores, she declined stating that she wasn't hungry. We ate at the dining table, talking and had family time.

***

In the evening I received a phone call from a nurse that I used to fuck back in the day. She worked at Loyola on the ICU unit. She informed me that Emani was stable and that the detectives were in the building. I told her to take care of something for me. After that I called to check on Emani's children making sure that they were doing fine. My soldiers told me that they were doing good and behaving. Since they were behaving I told them that they could put a 32inch flat screen in the room so that they could watch television. I could have a kind heart at times. The last thing that I wanted to do was kill Tyeisha and Lil Ty. At this point their lives were in the hands of their mother.

Chapter 30

Kenya

"I'm free!" I yelled as I jumped in the air like Mary Poppins. My little sister Kiara was crying as she waited for me to be released. She was the only person that came to visit me during my incarceration, never going a month without seeing me. When they transferred me from Chicago to Virginia Tavion made sure that Kiara still came to visit me. He would purchase her flight, book her room and give her spending money. Honestly Kiara was all that I had. When things got real in my family I had to step up. My mother was around but really wasn't a mom to me or Kiara. She was a selfish woman only providing for herself. My father was cool, always there for us. It was more like having a big brother at times. He would let me and Kiara do whatever we wanted to do as long as we finished high school. When I met Tavion I knew that he was the one. We clicked so fast and fell in love. Everything was fine till I caught a case and took the bid with him. While I was locked up things changed between us. Breaking up was the best thing for us to do. That still didn't stop us from being best friends.

"I miss you so much big sister." Kiara hugged me tightly. "Don't you ever leave me again." Kiara cried.

"I miss you more. Please stop crying before you make me cry." I wiped her tears away. "Let's get out of here." I followed Kiara to a white cute BMW 300. "Alright this is cute and fits you baby sister." I gave Kiara her props. My baby sister was a supervisor at M&M & Mars. I see that they were paying her good.

"Thank you. Wait till you see your new whip." Kiara slipped up saying. She used her hand to cover her mouth laughing.

"No way big mouth, tell me what type of car Tavion bought me." I begged her.

"No I'm not saying anything else." Kiara laughed. I started guessing different cars. Kiara ignored me laughing. She turned the radio up. Cardi B was rapping, *"You better be careful with me."* Kiara starting rapping. She hit the direction toward the expressway going south. I admired the changes within the last three years. Chicago was always fucking up shit and making things worst. Forty five minutes later we finally arrived to my new home. Kiara pulled up in front of a beautiful home whose landscaping was immaculate. She pulled into the driveway.

I got out of the car. "Tavion told me that he was going to look out for me, but I wasn't expecting this." I admired my new home.

Kiara dangled my house keys in her hand. "This belongs to you sister. Wait a minute, there's one more surprise."

The garage door opened. There was a candy apple red, new model Mercedes Benz C 300 with a big red bow on it. That wasn't only thing that brought me joy or that surprised me. Tavion stood by the Benz smiling dangling the car keys. "Welcome home Kenya baby." He smiled holding out his arms.

I ran to him jumping into his arms. "All of this is for me?" I asked him.

"Yes baby all 2,729 square feet of it. You haven't even seen the inside of the house yet." Tavion smiled.

"Thank you! Thank you! Thank you!" I kissed him. Tavion kissed me back softly. We both stared into each other eyes.

"Come on let's go and check out your new home Kenya." Kiara said snapping us out of our trance.

Tavion followed behind us as I walked inside my new home. The hardwood floors were beautiful. I had high vaulted ceilings with sunlight that shone through from God. My brick fireplace to keep me warm when the temperature drops in Chicago. My living room was furnished with a microfiber sectional and lovely coffee table. My dining room had a glass dining table that set six with turquoise accents to match my living room. I knew that Kiara did the decorating because she had my two favorite colors turquoise and gold. I had a large gourmet kitchen with a large island and plenty of counter space. It was large enough to eat in and had a wooden round kitchen table. The double staircase lead to the second level where there was a large loft and three bedrooms. All of them were furnished as well, my loft was set up as my office. My master suite had a huge walk in closet and private bath. I had four bathrooms, an attic and a finished basement with a full bath, large game room and kitchenette area. My backyard was open with a brick paver patio and scenic views.

"This is a dream come true. Not many women come home from jail to living like this unless they had a settlement against the state." I cried tears of joy and happiness.

Tavion rubbed my back, "You're special and deserve this and more." He wiped my tears away as we stood in the middle of my kitchen.

Pop! Kiara popped a bottle of champagne. We all laughed as she poured some in three glasses that sat on my granite counter. "One for you and you." She handed Tavion and me a glass. "A toast to celebrate new beginnings." We all tapped our glasses and begin to sip.

Kiara turned on the music while Tavion and I sat comfortably on my sectional. We all talked about what I've missed. Thirty minutes into our conversation my doorbell rang. *Ding, dong!* "I'll get that." Kiara hopped off from the sectional to answer the door.

To my surprised in walks "Dee, Dasia, Shay and Keith. "What's up sis! Welcome home!" They all screamed. Keith was the first person to give me a hug. "It's been a long three years sis. I miss you like crazy."

"I miss you too. So when are you going to let me meet your girlfriend?" I teased him. Keith would write me in jail all the time. In the letters he written about his girl Kamara.

"You'll meet her soon. I already told her so much about you." Keith told me.

Shay hugged me next. My friend was still grieving on the inside. Even though Jay isn't no longer here she still was family. Jay would fuck other chicks on the side, hell they all did in the past. However Shay had his heart and he was crazy about her. From the look in her eyes I could still see the pain. When I hugged her I felt it. "Shay how are you?" I asked her.

"I'm good, could be better. Never mind me, how are you?" she asked. Shay never liked attention. She was shy. When we met when I was a teenager, I would call her Shy Shay teasing her.

"I'm happy to be free." I replied.

Dee gave me a big hug. "I miss you so much." His big, strong muscles were squeezing the life out of me. "I miss you too brother. I'm sorry about what happened to Jay. That fucked me up when I heard what happened while I was inside."

"Sis I know, it fucked all us up." Dee replied. Dasia was standing right next to him. "I heard that you popped out two baby girls?! You don't look like it at all." I hugged Dasia.

"Girl let me show you the babies." Dasia, Shay, Kiara and I went to have a seat in the dining room. Dasia happily showed us pictures of her twin baby girls. The men sat in the living room discussing business. It was just like the old days. The whole gang was there except for Jay. Kiara poured everyone champagne except for Dasia, she declined because she was breastfeeding. While the girls were chatting Tavion and I locked eyes from across the room. He blinked at me while he continued to listen to the fellas. I blushed, smiling back at him. The girls caught our flirting action.

"I see someone is busy keeping you smiling." Dasia laughed.

"What are you talking about?" I giggled as I sipped on my champagne. "He's even finer."

"Such a shame that he's with Tichina now." Dasia whispered. Shay shot her a dirty look for saying that. Shay is my friend and played major roll in Tavion and me connection.

"Shay do you have a picture of her?" Normally I wouldn't be this messy but at a time like this I had to be. She showed me a picture of her, Dasia, Tichina and Kamara at Tavion's Grandmother Pearl house. I must admit that she was very beautiful, but she wasn't me. Shay noticed the look on my face.

"Kenya you're so rude, please give me a tour of your new home." She played it off.

"Girl my fault, let me show you around. Dasia would you love a tour as while?"

"Sure give me one second. Let me respond to one of my clients regarding a catering order and I'll catch up with yall upstairs." Dasia was in the process of making a phone call.

Shay, Kiara and I went upstairs for some privacy. My sister and I was ready to hear all the gossip on Tavion's new girlfriend. When we made it to my bedroom we step inside but cracked the door just a little. We all sat on the bed to get comfortable.

Shay kicked it off, "Girl I wrote you only so much because you know that they be reading your mail and shit. About Tichina, she's from out West, no children and a legal secretary or something. Anyway she met Tavion at their annual boat party and hooked up. She has two best friends, Kamara that's Keith new woman and Emani. I've only met Kamara, never Emani but that's the one behind all the setting up and bullshit."

"Right remember when I visited you sis and told you about the setup? That was who I was talking about, that Emani chick and her guy Tyrone." Kiara tried to explain to me.

"No his name is Ty, he's some nigga that supposedly been getting money from setting rich niggas up." Shay cleared up the confusion.

"Wait so you're telling me that Tichina's best friend Emani set up Jay to get killed?" I asked trying to make sense of everything.

"Exactly, Jay ass fucked Emani and they got his ass while in bed with her." Shay started to look sad.

"Shay I'm sorry to hear that." I gave my deepest apologies. We all know that Jay was the biggest hoe out of the group. We just never imagined that it would get him killed in life.

"Thanks. Mentally I've moved on my only concern is our beautiful daughter Jamila that we created. It's been kind of hard raising her alone without Jay. Money wise I was good because we prepared for moments like this. The hard part is Jamila asking for her father. She's clingy to Dee now more than ever."

"He's the closest thing to her father." I sadly replied.

"Right and their tight like glue. Unfortunately I have some bad news that's going to break Jamila's and Jay's heart." Shay looked away from me.

I looked at Kiara, my eyes asked her for some privacy. Kiara caught on leaving out of the room. Not that Shay and I was alone we could really talk. "Shay what's going on?"

Shay begin to cry. "Kenya I'm leaving Chicago. The plan was for Jay and me to leave in the first. Now that he's gone there isn't a reason for me to be here. I was offered a better paying job in California as Physical Therapist. I'm going to take it."

"That's awesome Shay! I remember when you struggled to put yourself through school. When you met Jay he feel so deep in love with you, that you had him paying your tuition the first week you met him. He'll want you to take that position."

"I know but Dee is going to be crushed when he hears that I'm moving." Shay replied. *Tap! Tap!* Someone tapped on the lightly. Shay and I both looked at the door. In walked Dee not waiting for me to invite him.

He looked at Shay. "Sis please don't take my Jamila away. She's all that I've got that's close to my brother." Dee begged her.

Shay stood up to him. "Dee I'm sorry that you had to find out this way. Please out of respect of Kenya and her home we can continue this discussion tomorrow."

"You're right. I apologize Kenya. Shay can you please come over my place tomorrow to continue this." Dee stared at Shay with sadness in his eyes.

"Jamila and I will be by your place sometime this week." She hugged Dee. In walked Dasia. Everyone was walking in at the wrong damn time.

"Is everything cool in here?" Dasia asked Dee. He took Dasia by the hand walking her out of the room. Dasia looked back at Shay and I in confusion. I shrugged my shoulders as if I didn't know what to tell her.

"Damn that was awkward. I was just trying to get my man back." I and Shay busted out laughing.

"Friend you're still crazy. Let's go downstairs and take care of that. You got to get that pussy ate and hit." Shay laughed.

We went back downstairs to where my small celebration was at. Music was playing, I noticed that we had pizza and hot wings. Yes finally food, that's what I missed the most. I walked over taking a seat next to Tavion on the sectional. He was chopping it up with Keith. Kiara bought us over food and more to drink. For the reminder of the day I laughed so hard with my friends who I considered family just like the old days. The sun was setting, it was starting to get dark. Everyone said their goodbyes before leaving my home. Everyone except for Tavion left. Now the real party was about to begin.

Chapter 31

Tavion

"I tried my best to make sure that I got everything that you asked for." Tavion said as we sat next to one another. "Wait I have to give you one more gift." Tavion led me upstairs to master bedroom. My pussy was happy than a mother fucker. "Hold up, were almost there." Tavion walked into my master closet opening up a hidden compartment in the back. "Come closer," he requested. I did what he asked me to do. Inside the hidden compartment was a safe. Tavion entered the safe code. When the safe popped opened I couldn't believe my eyes. There was stacks of money. "This is yours, all two hundred thousand." Tavion smiled. I started to cry touching the money. "You've always been a cry baby." Tavion hugged me. I buried my head into his chest. He still wore Tom Ford Oud Wood Intense cologne. That scent drove me wild. He kissed me softly, "I miss your ass Kenya.

"Tavion I miss you so much. I'm sorry about leaving you while I was inside. I was upset with you about a lot of things."

"Shhhh, it wasn't your fault. You had every fucking right to be upset and to leave. You owe me no apologies. I should be telling you that I'm sorry." Tavion said.

"Now is your chance." She told me.

I dropped to his knees. "Kenya please forgive me for putting you in a fucked up position which led to you serving my time. I'm sorry for taking away three years of your life. Can you find it in your heart to forgive me?" I looked up waiting for Kenya's response.

"Tee get up from off that damn floor. Yes. I forgave you a long time ago." She laughed.

I got up laughing. We both were feeling the liquor. Kenya went to turn on the water to the Jacuzzi and undressed. Damn she was beautiful, even badder than before she did that three year bid. Kenya body was filled out more places. Flat stomach, wide hips and big ass. Unlike them plastic surgery getting hoes, her thighs matched her round ass. My dick rose from the sight of her all her brown beautiness.

"So are you just going to stand there and stare at me? Or are you going to join me in the jacuzzi?" She laughed as the water flowed filling up the Jacuzzi.

"I was just taking the moment to enjoy the view." I smiled undressing.

Kenya got her thick ass into the Jacuzzi. I didn't waste any more time and joined her. She splashed water at me, *Splash!* "Oh you want to play?" I laughed splashing water back on her. When the water hit her face she giggled. At that moment that's how much I realized that I missed her laughed. I pulled her closer to me, "I still love you Kenya."

"I never stopped loving you Tavion." She said softly.

The look in her eyes were sincere. Here I was here with my first love while my woman was at home waiting for me. Tonight I was going to hurt them both. The selfish man in me was only thinking about himself, and worry about making things better with the both of them later. I lifted Kenya thick ass up sitting her on the edge of the jacuzzi.

She parted her juicy thighs opening them. I ran my fingers on her pussy lips. Kenya moaned as I fingered her pussy. She was soaking wet, dripping already down the insides of her thighs. I removed my fingers, they were glistening from her juices. I licked her juice off of them, she tasty so pure.

"I need to fill your mouth on my little wet pussy. Tavion I want to fill your fingers in me and your tongue on my clit. I want you to make me cum with your tongue and fingers like you used to do." Kenya begged.

"Open your legs wider for me. I want to taste you properly."

Kenya opened her legs widely. My mouth fell onto her pussy. I worked my tongue inside her, lapping greedily at the slippery juices oozing from her. She felt her first orgasm of the night start to rise deep within her as my tongue moved from inside her and to her swollen clit. I flicked my tongue gently and quickly. My fingers plunged back into her, fucking her. Instinctively she reached down and pulled my head firmly to her pussy.

"Yes. Just like that. Oh God. Oh yes, just like that." Kenya said as she fucked my mouth.

She gripped my head firmly. I pretended to try to pull away, but kept licking her clit and thrusting my fingers into her. I sucked on her click, tonguing it gently. Kenya shuddered, pushing my face deeper into her pussy. She wasn't sure if she wanted to cum or pee, but the feeling of my fingers and tongue were driving her insane.

"Come on my tongue." I managed to gasp.

I could feel her hips bucking. Kenya couldn't control her movements. She knew that I was finger fucking her but she simply couldn't tell exactly what I was doing to her clit that felt so incredible. All she knew was that she didn't want me to stop. Kenya gasped for breath and could feel the unstoppable surge of orgasm building like a great wave. Her pussy was throbbing and she knew she had to cum. Her surge of juices were flowing from her onto my fingers. I sucked on her pussy harder waiting on her explosion.

"Oh God, yes. Fuck. I am cumming." Kenya closed her thighs around my head. I lapped up her juices as they flowed from her. Her body was wracked by spasm after spasm. Then her legs opened releasing my head.

Kenya slipped down inside the jacuzzi with me. "I am so wet for you. I want you to fuck me now, I want you to fuck me deep Tavion." We went to her king size bed. She bends over waving her perfectly round ass in the air. I can't hold it anymore and slide my dick into her wet pussy.

"Oohh baby, I love how tight you are." I fucked her from behind, pressing her face into the pillows. Kenya's tight pussy was gripping my dick. "I don't want to bust, but it feels so fucking good."

"Nut if you need to honey. I can make you nut again. I promise." She moans.

"You want me to nut in you like this?"

"Yes please baby I need you to nut in me. "She starts to throw her ass back on my dick. I slam up into her, feeling her depths squeeze me.

"Oh fuck, I'm cumming!" she moans.

"That's right baby cum on that dick. Are you ready for mine?" She screams yes, and I join her in heaven.

Her contracting muscles brought on my own contractions, and now my powerful vein is pumping her with thick nut. My dick loves her. My dick showed how much that he missed her pussy. She lies on me for a while, until she starts to suck my dick and balls clean for me. She spends her time on my soft, still dick thick dick until she can't taste our sex anymore. As I laid there I didn't want to leave.

Ring! Ring! My phone starts blaring. "Yo, what's up?"

"Tichina is starting to get suspicious. She's called twice but I told her that you were busy getting our hands dirty." Keith informed me. I knew that if Tichina didn't hear from me that she would call him.

"Alright, I'm leaving now." I hung up and looked over at Kenya who was now sleep. I kissed her on the forehead waking her.

"I understand that you have to leave. I'll be here waiting on you Tavion. I love you."

"I'm not going anywhere. I'll be back, love you too. Get you rest." I smacked her on the ass before I got up.

By the time I cleaned myself up and got dressed she was indeed sleep. I let myself out and locked the door with the set of keys that I had. Once I got into my car I called Tichina. "What's up baby? I was handling something and couldn't talk at the moment."

"I know Keith told me. When will you be coming home? I miss you." Tichina sounded sad that I was gone all day.

"I'm on my way home to you now Queen."

"I'll be waiting up for you King, love you."

"I love you too baby. See you soon."

Thirty minutes later I made it home. Tichina didn't wait up for me. She was asleep, which played in my favor. I jumped in the shower thinking about how I was going to control my feelings for Kenya. When I got out the shower and laid next to Tichina the feelings that I had for Kenya faded away. Watching my baby Tichina sleep made me feel guilty that I fucked Kenya. I did exactly what I said I wasn't going to do. Now I was caught up in some bullshit.

Chapter 32

Emani

I woke up to a beautiful vase of red roses sitting on hospital table. I grabbed the Get Well soon card that was attached to it. It read: ***If you want to keep your children alive you better keep your mouth closed***. My blood pressure begin to rise on the machine. My children, oh God not my children. I winced in pain as I reached for the phone to call Big Momma.

"Hello Big Momma, are my children fine?" I anxiously asked her.

"No their not fine Emani. The other children said that two men came in the house taking them. Emani right now I just can't take any more of this madness. Your mother got to get buried, you're laid up in the hospital and now this. I'm going to call the police." Big Momma cried.

"No, please don't call them. I know who has them and they threaten to kill them if we get the police involved."

"Emani you better make sure that my grand babies don't get killed. Everyone around you is dying. Who's next? Something has to be done. Now I have to go up to Corbin's Funeral Home to make arrangements for your mom. One last thing before I go. I love you Emani, but when you're released out of the hospital you can't come back here." Big Momma cried.

"Alright Big Momma. I understand, please pray for me and my children. I love you."

"I'll never stop praying you and my grandchildren. I love and take care." Big Momma hung up the phone.

I cried alone in the hospital room with no one by my side. Big Momma was right, everyone was dropping around me. As far as my mother, fuck that bitch. She got what she deserved. If she wouldn't never set me up I wouldn't be in this damn hospital bed now. The pain from my shot wounds were getting worse. I pressed the call light so that I could ask for more pain medicine. All of this bullshit was stressing me out. Thoughts of them torturing my children filled my head. With the little strength that I had I got up to get the fuck out of there. My personal belongings were in the bag on the floor. I grabbed the bag searching for my phone. With the little juice that I had on my phone I ordered an Uber to take me home. Before leaving I took the medical supplies that were stocked up in my room. I pulled the IV out of my arm. Wearing a bloody hospital gown and socks I managed to elope out of Loyola. Trust me it wasn't an easy task. I had a lot of stares as I tried to blend in with everyone that was exiting the building. When I made it outside my Uber driver was parked out front. She didn't ask any question when I got inside. Quietly I sat in the back seat in pain till I arrived home.

When I made it home the pain was excruciating. The bandage on my side was soaked in blood and needed to be changed. While my phone was charging I changed my bandage. I snorted a line of cocaine and applied some to my wound to relieve my pain. The only thing on my mind was revenge. I had to get my babies back. God must've heard my prayers because I received an anonymous phone call from Dee.

"Aye bitch I heard that you eloped out of the hospital." He laughed, "You can run but you can't hide."

"Where are my babies?! You had better not touched them!" I warned him.

"You're not going to do shit if I do. You're lucky that I don't want to kill the, It's you that I want."

"I have cash. If it's money that you want. Please tell what I have to do to get my children back alive." I begged him.

"Don't you ever insult me like that again. I'll clean your money with my ass. If you want to see your children alive again, meet me at the warehouse."

Dee ended the phone call before I could say another word. I pulled my hair back into a ponytail. Slipped on some leggings and lastly put on my bullet proof vest before putting on my tee shirt. I made sure that my gun was fully loaded. My car was shot up so I had to Uber to Big Momma's house to grab my old Kia that was parked in her garage. The Uber arrived taking me to my destination. Thankfully I didn't have to go inside Big Momma's house. Instead I took the gangway to get to the back of the house. One of my little cousins was in the back waiting on me with the car keys.

"Thanks little cuz. Make sure that you don't tell Big Momma." I told her as I unlocked the car doors.

My little cousin had her right hand on her hip and her left hand out. "I won't as long as you pay me my money."

I laughed giving her the fifty dollars that I promised to pay her. She took the money and waited for me to pull out of the garage so that she could lock it back up. I drove to the warehouse in complete silence as I thought about my babies. When I arrived at the warehouse a black van was parked outside. I walked into the warehouse slowly with my hand on my gun. Dee and another younger man were inside.

"Where are my children?!" I asked him. Dee looked over at the young man and nodded his head. The younger man pulled my children from behind a steel machine. My children mouths were taped and hands were tied. Tears filled my eyes as I looked at how helpless they were.

Dee walked up to me. He stared into my eyes with so much hatred. If looks could kill I would've dropped dead. "I've been waiting on this moment." He raised his gun to my head.

My heart raced. It was time for me to meet my maker. He turned his back toward the young man. "Bring her children closer. I want them to watch me kill their mom." Dee said.

Now was the chance to grab my gun. Quickly I took it from my waist shooting Dee in the thigh as he turned back facing me. I took off running as fast as I could.

Pop! Pop! "I managed to hit the younger man in the shoulder. "Run Lil Ty!" I yelled as I dodged the bullets that were targeting me.

Lil Ty took off running with Tyeisha. Dee and the younger man chased after me trying to shoot me down. Bullets flew past my head and one caught me in the back slowing me down a bit. Lucky for me that I had on my vest. My children were out sight. I pray that they were able to get out of the warehouse alive. My shot wound started to bleed and my pain begin to raise. As I ran for my life I tripped over a steel pipe falling. Dee had an advantage over me now. No longer able to run I crawled under an opening hiding. Dee walked past me slowly.

"Come out bitch! You can only hide in here for so long!" he said as I watched his shoes walk pass me. Moments later the other man walked passed as well. I hid under the small space until I couldn't hear their footsteps or them breathing. When the coast was clear I sled from under the space running off slowly. I was bleeding profusely and felt as if I wanted to pass out. I ran through the warehouse until I seen sunlight. There was a door ahead which led you to the front of the warehouse outside.

"She's that way!" Dee told the young man. They both followed my trail of blood that I left behind.

"Help! Help!" I yelled as I ran outside of the warehouse. There wasn't anyone that could help me. A black Charger came speeding up the street. I jumped out in front of the car, "Help!" *Boom!* She hit me sending me flying in the air. I hit the ground landing on my back. From the pain in both of my legs I could tell that they were broken. Blood was pouring out of the back of my head. My vision was beginning to get blurry. The driver of the car got out screaming and crying hysterically.

"Oh my God! I'm about to call the ambulance. You came out of nowhere. I didn't see you." She cried.

Dee walked up pushing the woman out of the way. He pointed the gun at my temple. *Pop! Pop! Pop!* The woman took off running, got in her car and drove off. My life flashed before my eyes. Tyrese and Boogie appeared laughing wickedly at me. Damn, looks like I was joining them both in hell.

Chapter 33

Tichina

Six Weeks Later

Things at home we're starting to get back normal. The death of my former best friend fucked me up in the inside. Even though she betrayed me it hurt that she had to die like that. Now her two remaining children had to grow up without a mother and father. They will have to live with that for the rest of their lives. Tavion and everyone kept a low profile after all the deaths. We resumed our regular activities as such. Everyone that came for Tavion and his crew were all dead. It was sad that Tyshawn had to die because of his parents circumstances.

***

Tavion proved how much he loved me by his actions, but you know a woman intuition is a mother fucker. Since Kenya been released from the Fed's the smallest things have been off. For instance phone calls being taken in privacy. I hated that shit, normally he would talk business in front of me. Then he's been making runs that he doesn't explain. Where the fuck is he going that's so damn important? Lastly, he hasn't mentioned Kenya anymore. I know that she hasn't fallen off the planet. Inside my heart I felt that something wasn't right. Usually I would share this with Kamara, but she was going to tell me that I was tripping. Go on and on about how much Tavion loves me and blah…blah…blah. Right now Tavion was on another one of his runs. Once again I was in this big house alone with idle time on my hands. Now was the time for me to go through some of his personal belongings. He kept the huge safe down in the basement. I knew the combination to the safe. *"16, 24, 12."* I said out loud as I popped it opened. Inside the safe was stacks of cash, paperwork and keys that belonged to somethings that I didn't know of. Moving the cash to the side, I focused on the paperwork. It was a manila envelope that had 22996 Folkestone Way Mokena, Illinois. Curiously I opened up the manila envelope. The paperwork was a title with Tavion's name on it. There was also a deed stating that the property was now in Kenya's name. The date on title when he purchased the home was dated a month ago. We discussed Kenya coming home and how he had to look out for her, but why did he have to buy her a home that was close by. I took the folder with me and closed the safe

It only took me sixteen minutes to get to 22996 Folkestone Way from me and Tavion's place. When I pulled up Tavion's Maserati was parked outside in the driveway of the home. From the outside the home looked beautiful, but once I stepped inside things were going to get ugly. I rang the doorbell several times. ***Ding dong…Ding dong…Ding dong…*** The door opened up and appeared Kenya. She looked like her pictures except she was a little thicker. We both stared at each other before saying a word.

"Tichina pleas come inside." Kenya invited me inside as if she was expecting me. I stepped inside looking around for Tavion.

I turned to look at Kenya. "I hate that I have to meet you this way Kenya. Where is Tavion? He should be here for this meeting." I said.

"Please have a seat. Tavion went to go get my car checked out. It was making a knocking noise when I was driving so he took it back to the dealership. He should be back soon. Would you like something to drink? Wine, pop, tea or water?" Kenya asked.

"The only tea that I want from you is to know if you're sleeping with Tavion." I told her fake ass.

Kenya looked me with spite in her eyes. "Tichina I feel that you should ask Tavion that."

"Fuck that! I'm asking you. Are you and Tavion fucking? Yes or mother fucking no?" I was one second from smacking this dumb bitch.

Keys jingled in the front door locks. In walks the Head Nigga In Charge, Tavion. He didn't look surprised that I was here. I know that he seen my car that he bought parked outside. I shot him an evil stare. He took a seat next to me never making eye contact at Kenya. "Tichina what are you doing here?" He glanced over at the folder that I had in my hands. "You been in my safe snooping around?"

"I wouldn't have to snoop around if my man wasn't keeping secrets from me. Homes, cars, what else should I know Tavion?" I angrily asked him.

"Tell her everything that she needs to know." Kenya said with a sinister smile upon her face.

Tavion grabbed my hand as he prepared me for the bad news. "Kenya is pregnant with my child." He looked away in shame as he told me.

"No! No! No!" **Smack!** "You promised me that you wouldn't deal with her again. You lied about never having feelings for her! How could you do this to me Tavion!?"

"I didn't mean for all of this to happen. It happened all so fast." He lied to me.

"That's why you've been keeping everything a fucking secret. What are you going to do with the baby? I asked Tavion.

Kenya interjected, "We both decided to keep it."

I took one look at Kenya before leaping over Tavion punching her in the face. **Punch!** "You thirsty trap setting bitch!" Tavion pulled me off her trying to calm me down. I pushed him off of me. He landed on top of Kenya and I stormed out of her house. Tavion ran after me, but wasn't fast enough to catch me.

I drove home as fast as I could. When I got in I didn't go crazy. I didn't pack my shit or destroy anything. Instead I poured myself a glass of Hennessy and sipped that shit straight. There was no reason to make my blood pressure go up. Moments later Tavion made it home looking stupid and shit. He tried to hug me. "Don't you dare touch me?" I warned him.

"Tichina, she doesn't have to keep the baby. I'll stop seeing her, you just say the word." Tavion had the nerve to say.

"Oh so now it's up to me? You fuck and pop your ex bitch off! Put me at risk to get a sexually transmitted disease. Then you say that it's up to me if she keeps your baby. You ain't shit Tavion!"

"You don't have to worry about getting shit. You know me better than that."

"Tavion I thought that I knew you, but apparently I don't know you at all. You disgust me. I thought that you were different." I took a sip of my Henny.

"I'm going to make an appointment for the abortion clinic." Tavion pulled out his cellphone.

I pushed his cellphone down. "You don't have to do that. Honestly I think it's best that she keeps the baby. After all, she'll be giving you something that I could never give you. A child." Tavion held me in his arms as I cried. "Have your baby, but you can't deal with her again. No feelings, no sex, nothing. After the baby is born she has to sign over her rights to you and me."

"Kenya won't fall for that Tichina." Tavion replied.

"Trust me she will. She vindictive and malicious. She doesn't want to be a mom. She's only pregnant to gain you back. But that's not going to happen because I'm not ending things with you. Not unless that's what you want to do."

"Tichina I never want to stop being with you. I fucked up and I promise to never fuck up again. I'm sorry about hurting you."

"No matter what has happened. No matter what you've done. No matter what you and her will do. I will always love you." I cried.

Chapter 34

Sunshine

It's been eight days since I've been released from the hospital after extensive rehabilitation. Instead of going back to Aunt Marci's place. I went to live with Duke's mom. Mrs. Rice offered her guest room to me. It was safer to live with them in the suburbs than on the west side. I heard about everything that went down with Tyrese, Emani, Maine, Sweety and Tweety. I didn't feel safe laying my head in the hood. I was happy that Tyrese was dead. All the charges against me for Duke's death were dropped. Detective Carr said that they didn't have enough evidence against me.

***

Mrs. and Mr. Rice home was lovely. The guest room on the first floor was set up for me accommodating my needs. Mrs. Rice made sure that I didn't have to go up and down the stairs for anything. There was also a full bathroom on the first level. It felt good to be walking again, with the help of my walker of course. Mrs. Rice enjoyed my company because Mr. Rice was never really at home. I never questioned where her sixty three old husband whereabouts were. That wasn't my business. Mrs. Rice would cook for me and buy me things. She treated like I was her daughter. I truly appreciated it because I never had a mother.

At night I had crazy dreams which had me to toss and turn all night. Duke would come to me in my dreams. It felt as if we were together. It was surreal as if he was here. I would wake up in the middle of the night in a pool of sweat. I never shared this with Aunt Mari or Mrs. Rice. I didn't want them to start freaking out. It's a possibility that it could be all the medication that I could be taking. One of those medications caused nightmares. I thought that if I stopped taking the medication that the nightmares would stop, but they never did. Duke still continued to come to me in my dreams.

Today I was experiencing shortness of breath and chest pains. The chest pains could be from the unhealthy food that I could be eating. I couldn't explain the shortness of breath. By the evening both were gone and I was feeling better. Mrs. and Mr. Rice went out to dinner leaving me alone. I cooked myself dinner, ate and enjoyed a movie on Netflix. It was after nine pm so I decided to go to sleep.

In the morning Mrs. Rice knocked on the bedroom door. It was after ten am, normally I would've been up by now. When I didn't answer her, she entered into the bedroom. She tried to wake me up by shaking me. She noticed that something was right and checked my pulse. When she couldn't hear my pulse, quickly she started to perform CPR on me. Unfortunately for me it was too late. I was already dead. The coroner said that my cause of death was sleep apnea. I stopped breathing in my sleep.

The End

The Conclusion

Tavion & Tichina

Tavion and Tichina we're still together. The judge granted them both rights of Tavion's son. Tavion named his son after him. Tichina loved his son as her own, but still wanted her own child. They tried In vitro fertilization several times, but was unsuccessful. Tavion asked Tichina both got married.

Kamara & Keith

Kamara had another baby girl naming her Karah. Karlie was so happy that she was a big sister. Karlie wrote two children's book with the help of her mom. Keith and Kamara got married and lived happily ever after.

Dasia & Dee

Dasia and Dee moved out of Chicago. It was nothing but bad memories there. Dasia's mom convinced them to move to Arizona. Dee would visit his twin brother Jay's grave every year on his birthday. The change of scenery was great for their family. They opened up a very successful Chicago Cuisine restaurant. They both got married and lived happily ever after.

Kenya

After several unsuccessful attempts to get back with Tavion, Kenya signed her parental rights over to Tavion. She wasn't ready to have a child or wanted to be a single mother. She met another man and they both fell in love with one another. Tavion allows her to see her son whenever she likes.

Shay

Shay moved to California accepting the higher paying Physical Therapist position. Her decision was best for her and Jay's daughter Jamila. She always sent Jamila to Arizona for the summer to visit her uncle Dee and aunt Dasia. Shay met a Sports Physician, got married and had a son.

Bridget

Bridget and her three sons moved out of Chicago never looking back. Her new home was Atlanta. They liked the South much better. Bridget went back to school for Accounting and Payroll which led her to get a better paying career. Her sons grew up and went to college. She gave up on love until she met an older man who married her and spoiled her like she wanted.

Big Momma

After burying her daughter and granddaughter, Big Momma put her home up for sale. She raised Emani's children and they moved down South. She always wanted to move to North Carolina to be close to her sisters. She still went to church, played bingo and kept her diabetes under control. Lil Ty and Tyeisha liked North Carolina. They grew up being the opposite of their parents both excelling academically in school and received full scholarships for college.